The Diet

Also by Edita Kaye

Fiction
> *The Diet*

Nonfiction
> *The Calcium Diet*
> *Cooking Skinny*
> *Skinny Rules*
> *The Skinny Pill*
> *The Fountain of Youth*
> *Bone Builders: Complete Lowfat Cookbook Plus Calcium Health Guide*
> *Managing And Marketing A Refractive Surgery Practice*

The Diet

This book is a work of fiction. Names, characters, places and incidents are products of the author's imagination or are used fictitiously. Any resemblance to actual events or business establishments, locales or persons living or dead, is entirely coincidental.

Copyright © 2005 by Edita Kaye
All rights reserved. This book, or parts there of, may not be reproduced in any form without written permission. For information address: The Wave Group, Inc. Wave Books 830-13 A1A North, Ponte Vedra Beach, FL 32082.

Visit *The Diet* Website at
www.dietnovel.com

ISBN: 0-9740955-2-4

Library of Congress Cataloging-in-Publication Data
Kaye, Edita
    The Diet/Kaye, Edita—1st ed.
    1. Reducing Diets—Fiction. 2. Weight loss--
Fiction. 3. Cookery—Fiction. 4. Cooks—Fiction.

Library of Congress Control Number: 2004111477

Second Printing

Printed in Canada

The Diet

A Novel

Edita Kaye

Wave Books
The Wave Group, Inc.

The Diet

For Mark

The Diet

Contents

Prologue	11
Part One	13
Part Two	133
Part Three	249
Author's Note	272

The Diet

For Your Body

"Life itself is the proper binge."—Julia Child

For Your Mind

"You must do the thing you think you cannot do."—Eleanor Roosevelt

For Your Spirit

"When I stand before God at the end of my life, I would hope that I would not have a single bit of talent left and could say, 'I used everything you gave me.'"—Erma Bombeck

Diet
(dī′∂t) n. Greek diaita,
A way of life

The Diet

Prologue

"What a blimp."

"We're goin' to need another two guys just to lift her up."

"The cop said she's got a couple of kids. Can you imagine making love to that?"

"Looks like she ate herself to death."

"Shut it."

The voices, young, male, insensitive, fell silent. The command came from their boss, the chief of the rescue unit. He looked pointedly toward the doorway. There, on the threshold, stood twelve-year old Cate holding her five-year old sister Sam by the hand. They watched as the ambulance men squatted around the body of their mother lying dead on the kitchen linoleum.

"Toss me that blanket," snapped the chief.

"A blanket ain't goin' do it. We're gonna need a parachute," whispered a pimply youth.

"How about a tent?" another shot back under his breath.

The Diet

"I told you to put a lid on it," the chief ordered, his voice like ice. But his eyes, as they met Cate's large frightened ones, were warm and compassionate.

The snickering stopped. They crowded in, blocking her view. All Cate saw was a dark blue fence of uniforms. All she heard was the crunch of boots on broken cookies and the soft sucking sound when they stepped into the puddle of melting chocolate and marshmallow ice cream.

"Easy," directed the chief. "All together now, on the count of three. One. Two. Three. Lift." A choked-off curse, a last muffled grunt, and they were gone.

Cate looked at what was left of her mother. Just cookie crumbs, ice cream stains, an overturned bowl of cold spaghetti, and hundreds of diet books that had toppled from their shelves as her mother clutched at them to break her fall. But they didn't save her.

Cate knew deep inside herself that the men spoke the truth. Her mother did eat herself to death. Something in her heart hardened against her mother. Standing there in the mess of junk food her mother couldn't resist, and the ruined promise of so many diet books, Cate whispered a vow under her breath. "I will never be fat."

Sam looked up at her older sister and solemnly repeated Cate's vow in her small child's voice.

The promise, *I will never be fat*, vibrated through every fiber of Cate's being, even as the lady from children's services came and took her and Sam away.

The Diet

Part One

The Diet

Chapter 1

Cate hated her body, her fat and herself.

"How could I have gained almost ninety pounds in just one year?" she asked her reflection in the darkened window. "How could I have gone from one-hundred-and-fifteen pounds and a size six to two hundred pounds in this plus size?"

She looked down at her swollen and shapeless body and remembered another kitchen twenty years before and another body bloated with fat.

"How could I have turned into my mother?"

But nobody answered. Cate was completely alone.

It was almost midnight. An October wind blew the first leaves of fall down the deserted street. The neighborhood was quiet. The houses slept.

"I've still got you, don't I?" she asked the fridge. "You won't leave me, will you?"

She opened the freezer compartment and pulled out her second pint of chocolate chip ice cream.

The Diet

She had already finished off half a loaf of white bread and most of a jar of strawberry jam. But it wasn't enough. She needed more. She had to have more.

Because this was the night Cate had decided to finally end it all, and eat herself to death.

Chapter 2

Death by carbs was not such a bad way to go, she decided, adding a family-size bag of cookies and the remains of some stale potato chips to her kitchen table buffet.

Alternating mouthfuls of chips, ice cream and cookies, she still couldn't satisfy the cravings that tortured her. She couldn't stuff the sweet and salty junk food into her mouth fast enough to soothe the food demons raging inside.

"Pizza, that's what I need to finish the job faster," she thought. "Pizza and those killer cinnamon buns with the thick white dipping frosting."

After all, she needed all the edible weapons of self-destruction available.

She had the number to the pizza place on speed dial.

"Hi," she could barely control the need in her own voice. "Can you send three large pepperoni pizzas and three orders of those cinnamon buns? Thank you. What? Yes, I've got a real hungry crowd here," she said, looking around the empty kitchen. "Twenty minutes? That's great."

This is what she had become.
A food liar.
A food addict.
And a food balloon.
But she hadn't always been like this.
No, she hadn't always been like this.

Chapter 3

Could it have only been just last year? She had been very different then, Cate remembered.

On this night a year ago, Cate had been slim and sleek in a fitted white sweater and pencil-thin charcoal skirt cinched tightly at the waist with a narrow leather belt.

She had worn her long dark-brown curly hair high on her head to reveal her slender neck and add a slightly vain inch to her five-foot-five inch frame.

There were small gold hoops in her pierced ears and a square watch with a cowhide band on her wrist. Her nails had been short on her long fingers. She had worn no rings—not even a wedding band—to distract from the food she prepared every day.

Last year's Cate had sat at this very kitchen table and nibbled delicately on one of the black olives she fished out its bath of wine vinegar, olive oil and razor-thin slices of lemon. She had picked at a sliver of milky-white veal, and played with a curl of golden grilled sweet pepper fragrant with herbs.

The Diet

And last year's Cate wasn't alone. She had a husband who was on his way home to her, and she had wonderful news to share.

Last year's Cate had been fit and lean, in control of her body and her life.

"Look at me now," she said to herself, disgusted.

This year's Cate strained the buttons of a size eighteen top, and her stomach rolled over the elastic waistband of a pair of plus-size pants.

Her hair was lank, just pulled back with an old scrunchie. She had long since put away the slim watch, which had become too tight for her wrist, and the tiny hoops that now seemed ridiculous because somehow, even her ears looked fatter.

This year's Cate waited not for a husband to come up the drive, but only for the kid who delivered the pizzas.

This year's Cate was a two hundred pound out-of-control carb addict waiting for a triple order of pizza and those cinnamon buns with white sugar frosting she couldn't resist.

As she waited, she asked herself for the umpteenth time how, in just twelve short months, could she have packed on so much fat? And how, in the process, did she lose her shape, her husband, her family and her whole future?

The answer came back as it always did, "One mouthful at a time."

Chapter 4

It was true. She lost her perfect life to food.

What an irony. Food had given her that perfect life in the first place.

She had been *the* Cate, of *Cate's Cookery*.

Part studio, part classroom, part café, it was the most exciting shop for gourmets and food lovers in the state. "Foodies" had even started to travel the sixty miles from New York City to purchase *The Cookery's* private label foods and to take Cate's cooking lessons.

For Cate had the gift of food. She made the exciting, simple. The exotic, attainable.

She did it all with imagination, style and flair.

In addition to running *Cate's Cookery* she also wrote a cooking column in *The Record*, the town's newspaper, and had a weekly food segment on a local television station.

Her innovative recipes and her reputation were beginning to spread beyond the small upstate New York town. Cate was developing a presence. She was becoming known.

The Diet

She was blessed in other ways, too. She had her handsome husband Charles who, after much struggling, was on his own way to fame and fortune as a partner in a growing high-tech company.

And she had her baby sister, Sam, now a beautiful, slim young woman, who was learning the business of food right along side Cate in *The Cookery*.

Cate had everything, except a child.

Then her prayers were answered.

Another blessing would be granted her. She was to have a baby. She and Charles would become her dream family at last.

And so it was on that first October night, just one year earlier, Cate was in the same kitchen, preparing the dinner that she thought would celebrate the start of their family and the crowning gift to her enviable life.

But instead it would mark the end.

Chapter 5

"When will that pizza get here?" she thought, impatiently checking the wall clock. "They said twenty minutes." Then she realized only two minutes had elapsed since she first placed her order.

Cookies and ice cream gone, desperate to quell the need for the sweet, soothing carbs her body demanded, Cate reached into the garbage and fished out a tangle of cold spaghetti she had discarded earlier. She dumped the strands into a bowl, smeared lumps of cold butter over them, added a few heaping spoonfuls of sugar and a couple of shakes of cinnamon.

"Not quite cinnamon buns, but it'll do until the real thing gets here," she thought.

Just as she was carrying the bowl to the table the phone rang. Her mouth full of spaghetti and sugar she read the caller ID—*The River Hills Record*. That meant Josh—again.

"Why can't he leave me alone?" she moaned.

Then she remembered. Josh never gave up. Not on a story and not on a person. That was what she had loved about him. Like a gas flame he burned hot and clean and beautiful.

Not like Charles. Her husband was more like the flat element on an electric stove, slow to warm, slow to cool, and between those two states gave off uneven heat.

Then she felt guilty at her disloyalty and ate another mouthful of her spaghetti dessert to make herself feel better.

The phone kept ringing. Then finally, blessed silence.

"Thank God for voice mail," Cate sighed, as she saw the red message light begin to blink.

It reminded her of another flashing red light on the night Josh first crashed into her life eight years before.

She was stopped at a railway crossing on a wet, foggy night when his Jeep water-planed on the slick road, skidded and slid into the back of her car.

"Are you okay?" Those words of concern were the first words Josh had ever spoken to her.

More shaken than hurt, Cate had just nodded as she inspected the damage to their car, which neither she nor Charles could afford to fix. They were both out of work and almost out of gas money.

"Look, I've got to cover a story," Josh had explained, fishing a business card out of the pocket of his jeans.

"There's a bad pile-up on the other side of that overpass. As soon as I'm done we'll take care of your car. Don't worry."

The Diet

But she was worried, and must have looked scared to death, because the next thing she knew he was holding open the door of his Jeep and saying, "You can't stay out here alone. Come on, get in."

Something about his longish hair, a little gray at the temples, his strong mouth, and the warmth in his eyes, reminded her for an instant of the man who had looked at her so kindly the night her mother had died.

"Come on. Get in," Josh repeated.

And she did.

Sitting in the front seat of his car, she watched him work. It might have been a small town and it might have been a small-town paper, but there was nothing small about Josh. He knew his stuff. He was good.

Later, as they waited together for the tow truck, they sipped bitter gas station coffee and talked.

She learned that his was the first family to clear land in what was now the town of River Hills, a high-end bedroom community on the shores of the Hudson River. She learned that his great-grandfather was the first mayor of the town, that his grandfather and father were town selectmen, and that he, Joshua Nathaniel Cody, was the owner of *The River Hills Record*, established by his family over one hundred years ago.

Josh had roots, and they went deep.

He was easy to talk to. She found herself confiding in him. She told him how she and her husband Charles and her younger sister, Samantha—Sam—had just arrived from a small rural town on the most northern border of

Connecticut, the fifth such town they had tried to settle down in. She told him that Charles had just lost another job, and with a flash of pride, that she had recently completed a correspondence degree in journalism.

By the time the tow truck arrived, Cate had a check in her pocket that would more than cover the repairs to the old car and even fill the tank with gas. She also had her first job as a journalist. She was to be the newest staff writer for *The River Hills Record*.

The Diet

Chapter 6

Josh had started out as her boss and then became her mentor and finally her friend.

And she had let him down.

It was Josh who had first appreciated her extraordinary gift with food. For six months, he sampled the goodies she brought into the office almost daily.

She made a panade, an aromatic soup of leeks, celery, sorrel and cream-soaked cubes of French bread simmered in hot milk, thickened to creamy custard consistency with eggs and finished with nutmeg.

She brought in a dish made with cold lamb, chopped eggs, olive oil, lemon juice and Worcestershire sauce, stirred into a creamy mustard base and garnished with fresh mint.

She baked pink and green tartlets filled with pale grape custard and flaky triangles of pastry stuffed with either spiced apples or homemade mincemeat or dollops of sweet mango glazed with a wash of egg white and ground sugar.

One day he called her into his office and told her that she should combine her twin talents—cooking and writing—together in one career.

He pushed her to study culinary arts at night and even helped with her tuition, calling it an investment in his newest writer. His graduation gift to her was the first public recognition she ever had, a column of her own.

He hadn't stopped there.

He arranged an interview with the local television station that had turned into a weekly food segment.

Finally, and most importantly, it was Josh who had believed in her enough to convince the landlord to give her the lease on what would become *The Cookery*.

Now she was repaying him with silence and shame.

The phone rang again, interrupting her memories. It was Josh again and again she let it go into voice mail.

It didn't ring again.

But the silence was worse.

It quickly filled up with the pounding of Cate's heart and the rapid spinning of her thoughts.

As she waited for her pizza, she ate the rest of her junk food and thought about the food she used to make.

Inventive hors d'oeuvres, succulent roasts, surprising salads brimming with exotic lettuces and herbs, golden soufflés, light-as-air desserts, warm fragrant breads, preserves: all those wonderful recipes had given her such success.

She thought about her columns, her television segments and her exquisite shop, *The Cookery*.

Food had made all her dreams come true. Then, last year, food turned her life into the nightmare it was now.

It all began on what she believed would be the most completely perfect day of her life.

Chapter 7

On the morning of that beautiful October day, a light sprinkling of early frost powdered the lawns and the autumn sun rose like a huge golden pumpkin.

Cate was in the bathroom, too excited to even breathe, praying for the tiny blue sign that would mean she was finally pregnant.

"How absolutely right," she thought, reading the instructions on the pregnancy test packet, "that the sign for a baby should be a little plus sign, a little cross. Because that's exactly what our child will be, an addition *and* a blessing."

As she waited, wishes and prayers swirled around her head like the mass of dark curly hair that always escaped her antique silver clip.

To distract herself, she checked her make-up for the fifth time in as many minutes. A little mascara just on the tips of her lashes to bring out her dark blue, almost navy eyes; a sweep of rose blush to heighten her already beautiful cheekbones and a dash of lip gloss to shine her smile into brilliance.

The Diet

She pinned on a silver rose brooch and smoothed her straight skirt over her slim hips. Still in stocking feet, all she needed was to slip into her pumps, grab her trench coat, bag and phone and she would be ready to start the day.

"Please," she whispered to the mirror and checked her watch again. "Please let it be a baby."

She had been ready for a baby for a long time. Her career at *The Record* was solid. Her television segments were beginning to attract local sponsors. *The Cookery* was in the black and making a small profit. And she was in her early thirties, not to young, not too old.

But Charles, always cautious, had urged patience.

It was always like that between them. Cate craving change, growth and new challenges and Charles preferring to stand still on the spot he knew rather than to move forward into the new or unknown.

They balanced each other from the moment they met.

Cate Blaine and Charles Churchill were barely in their teens when they first met. Both had lost their fathers when they eight-years old and then, a few years later, their mothers. Loss had been the first bond between them.

Even at that trembling age on the brink of womanhood, Cate was already a beauty with flashes of the drive and ambition that would be so evident later.

Charles had reached the full height of a man, more gangling than lean, but while his body developed his face still had the soft features of childhood.

The Diet

Cate and Sam living in and for each other, hardly noticed the succession of foster homes they had been placed in or the succession of foster mothers who ran them.

Charles, on the other hand, had been in just one foster home run by a substitute sixth-grade teacher.

Mrs. Beatrice French, a childless widow, was in her fifties, with the scrawny bony frame that almost always ensured long life and a sharp mind. Her gray hair was cut in a no-fuss short bob. She wore no makeup, no sunscreen and no nail polish.

She was never still. If she wasn't correcting schoolwork, she was mending or knitting.

She wasn't a complete throwback. Her living room contained a television and even a VCR. But the channel was always set to an educational program and the movies were mostly traditional classics.

Mrs. Bea, as she was called, lived a black-and-white life.

At first she had several boys in her care, but over the years accepted fewer and fewer, until just Charles was left.

While she had no love in her to give to him, she did offer security, and he felt safe in her never-changing house.

When Cate and Sam moved in next door, Charles became their constant companion. He adored the electric pulse that vibrated in Cate, and she loved the steady glow of constancy that ran through Charles.

The Diet

And so, lacking any real family, they adopted each other and with Sam created a kind of family of their own.

Charles settled into the pattern of their lives. Cate, exhausted by trying to be both mother and father to Sam, clung to him.

But then life changed for them, as life always does.

Chapter 8

Cate's winning a college scholarship marked the first change in their relationship.

Charles panicked and begged her not to go. He quit high school, found a job and bought her a ring.

Cate, torn between the new challenge and the overwhelming aloneness of her responsibility to Sam, chose Charles. And so, still in their teens, they got married.

They had a one-day honeymoon in a roadside motel with Sam asleep on a foldout cot.

For a wedding present, he brought her brochures and an application for a correspondence course.

They rented a two-room walk-up above a hardware store, and the three of them began to play house for real.

But Cate, unable to suppress her nature, soon grew restless with menial part-time jobs and wanted something better for herself, for Sam and for Charles.

To give him credit, Charles tried. He took computer training. He applied for and got a better job. And then he lost it. He got another and lost that.

The Diet

They moved to a new town and moved again. Then again.

Cate always took his side against his employers. She supported him, first with love and understanding, and as soon as she was able, with money. But no matter how hard he tried success eluded him.

Then four years ago it seemed as if luck and timing finally came together to give Charles the success he desired.

The high-tech business he started with four buddies he had met taking courses at night had struggled on the brink of disaster. Year after year, Cate and *The Cookery* provided some financial stability and a home for the three of them until finally Charles came home glowing with news. They had landed their first major contract. The company was on its way.

That night they began to make plans for a baby.

Chapter 9

"Just a few minutes more," Cate thought impatiently as she checked her watch again, waiting for the test results.

She tried to distract herself by planning the cooking lesson she would give to her morning class.

She couldn't decide between the craft of creating profiteroles, cream puffs stuffed to bursting with a cream filling and drenched in bittersweet chocolate or whipping up a big bowl of Zabaglione, thick and golden with country egg yolks and sugar laced with Marsala and her own added touch, melted semi-sweet chocolate. Maybe they would make both.

"Okay. This is it," she whispered, unable to wait any longer. She closed her eyes, crossed her fingers and started counting down the last ten seconds.

"Mississippi one, Mississippi two, Mississippi three…" Then she peeked. There on her bathroom counter, shiny in its white plastic case, shimmered a miniature bright blue cross.

She was pregnant.

The Diet

"I'm going to be a mother," she suddenly realized.

In that instant, a heavy cloud dimmed the sun. The golden light turned gray.

Cate's face swam and shifted and the image of her mother's white face and grossly obese body swam into the mirror. She shivered with a sudden foreboding and felt a heart-squeezing stab of terror.

Then just as suddenly as it had appeared, the cloud blew past. Sunlight skipped across the mirror, chasing away the shadows and warming her. Her shivering stopped and her heart beat normally again.

Cate looked at the little blue cross and drew strength from it.

"I'm going to be a mother," she whispered, and pushed the ugly pictures of her own mother deep down into her most secret place, not realizing that they lay dangerously close to the new flickering life of her baby.

The Diet

Chapter 10

"Good morning. This is Cate Churchill. I'd like to make an appointment with Dr. Selig," she said to the answering service operator. "Can you please tell him it's for a prenatal? I'm pregnant."

She couldn't help it. She was full of joy, bursting with it. She had to share her news with everyone, even the bored-sounding operator, everyone—except Charles. She would wait until tonight and surprise him.

As she drove to *The Cookery,* she thought about the dinner she would make to celebrate. She would cook Italian, she decided, for luck.

They had spent the first hours of their brief honeymoon as armchair travelers, pouring over big illustrated books of Italy in a bookstore while Sam sat cross-legged across the aisle, listening to a children's story hour.

Their wedding dinner was in a small neighborhood Italian restaurant. They celebrated the first chapter of their life together over big bowls of steaming pasta tossed

The Diet

simply with fresh garlic and olive oil and buried under a snowstorm of grated Parmesan and Romano cheeses.

The owner set out platters of spiced olives, rounds of Italian sausage glistening with fat, charred wedges of broiled red pepper and a cutting board with a worn knife and warm loaf. There was more of the rich olive oil for dipping the bread, and they ate and laughed and kissed, their lips slick and oily.

Sam sat at the head of the table, sipping apple juice out of a balloon wine glass, spilling meatballs and marinara sauce everywhere.

Italian had been lucky for them. Cate hoped that it would be lucky again.

The Diet

Chapter 11

Navigating carefully through the still sparse morning traffic, she thought about her menu for this most special dinner.

She already had jars of Charles' favorite, shiny black and green olives marinated in oil and red wine vinegar seasoned with garlic and the sharp tang of lemon. She would serve those as a starter with a crusty loaf of Italian bread, soft and white on the inside and golden and crunchy on the outside. She would set out a shallow dish of pale olive oil, with a swirl of dark balsamic vinegar, for dipping chunks of the bread.

The first course would be a creamy fettuccine Alfredo made of fresh pasta rich with cream, butter and cheese.

She decided on Saltimbocca à la Romano for the main course. For the ingredients, she had to pull off into the market.

It didn't take her long to select paper-thin slices of salty prosciutto and leaves of fresh sage to be placed on top of delicate strips of milky-white veal pounded to paper thinness. She would brown each piece of the veal, prosciutto and sage combination in unsalted butter and then pour a rich, red vermouth over it and let it soak. Hot, sweet, and dripping with butter and wine, the veal dish was a classic.

She also added a few red and yellow peppers and two purple onions to roast as a side dish.

Next she bought a pint of heavy cream. Lavishly sweetened with sugar and flavored with the essence of almonds, the cream would be whipped into soft peaks. She would float big spoonfuls into cups of the strong black coffee Charles loved.

The only thing left to decide was dessert. News like hers called for something very special.

It came to her at the checkout counter. She would make what was known as Cate's Celebration Cake. It was her signature dessert, elegant and beautiful. It was the perfect choice.

Chapter 12

Pleased with her dinner menu, she was just two blocks from *The Cookery* when her cell phone rang.

"Mrs. Churchill? This is Dr. Selig's office," said a firm, professional voice. "Dr. Selig got your message and would like you to come in as soon as possible."

Before she could respond, the voice continued, "Can you come in this morning—say in about thirty minutes?"

The day suddenly got darker and colder. Cate was gripped by a second wave of fear. She must have said yes but she didn't hear herself. All she could hear was the rush of panic in her ears.

"Something's wrong. Why does he want to see me right away?" and she worried as she pulled over to the side of the road.

"Don't imagine things," she instructed herself as she tried to talk her fears away.

"Dr. Selig has been my doctor for years, ever since we moved here to River Hills. He knows how much I've wanted a baby," she thought to herself. "I always mention it whenever I see him. He probably just wants to congratulate me before the office gets too filled up with patients," she rationalized. "Or perhaps he had a sudden cancellation or maybe he's going out of town or on vacation and wants to see me before he goes."

But none of the maybes calmed her rapid pulse or soothed her deepening anxiety.

With her heart clamped tight in a ball of fear, Cate started the car and turned it toward the doctor's office.

Chapter 13

"Calm down Cate, and listen to me carefully. You know there's a history of hypertension, cardiovascular disease, diabetes and obesity in your family. I called you in just to take some routine tests and get them out of the way," Dr. Selig explained, meeting Cate's eyes.

Dressed again, she perched on the very edge of a leather wingback chair crowded against the front of a massive partners' desk that filled up most of the space in his small consulting room.

She knew, of course, who he meant when he talked about "family history" and once again the image of her mother floated across her vision.

Dr. Selig continued, "You're my special lady so stop worrying. Just relax. You are going to be a wonderful mother, and you are going to have a beautiful healthy baby. I'm going to take very good care of you both."

Cate tried to find reassurance in his words but he couldn't mask the concern in his eyes or the tension in his voice. She knew he was worried.

The Diet

"I'll get back to you just as soon as I get the test results." With a friendly squeeze of her shoulder and a final, "Don't worry," he was gone.

Chapter 14

A few minutes later Cate was back in her car.

"Dr. Selig is right," she told herself. "There's nothing to worry about."

She took a deep cleansing breath, rolled her shoulders to dispel some of the tension that had settled at the base of her neck, and reached for the thermal mug still half-full of her aromatic breakfast coffee.

"What's the matter with you?" she scolded herself. "Caffeine is a no-no. No more coffee. From now on it's herbal tea." She rolled down the window and poured out the rest of the coffee.

She immediately felt better and back in control.

It was time to get to work. She was already late for *The Cookery*.

As she started the engine, she glanced at herself in the car mirror.

"Do I look any different now that I'm pregnant?" She wondered, "Do I have that glow everyone talks about?"

But the face looking back at her was the same.

The Diet

Chapter 15

Cate opened the door and the magic happened once again.

The last tiny splinters of worry dissolved as she turned on the lights, and *The Cookery* came alive.

Following a ritual she had begun the day she signed the lease and opened those doors for the first time, Cate walked slowly through the space, lightly touching all her favorite things and counting all her blessings.

She had filled *The Cookery* with everything she loved. It home to her talent and her spirit.

A massive pine dresser stood against one wall straining under an eclectic collection of antique china: lettuce-leaf salad plates, bluebell teacups edged in gold, a whimsical cream jug in the shape of Cinderella's slipper as well as vintage toffee tins.

An old washstand Cate had rescued from a garage sale hid its battered doors behind bright cotton skirts printed with fat cabbage roses. Standing gloriously on top was a pitcher overflowing with baby's breath.

The Diet

Tall bookcases filled with cookbooks flanked an overstuffed easy chair and a bentwood rocker, forming a cozy corner.

One wall was covered with fruit. A sparkling strawberry, wet with dew, was captured in oils. An unframed photograph of an apple, in deepening shades from soft celadon to mellow gold, was propped against a slightly frayed and faded tapestry of grapes and pheasant.

The entire back wall was glass. Two floor-to-ceiling French doors opened onto a courtyard rimmed with stone pots overflowing with fresh herbs, miniature tomato plants and flowers.

Fitted glass shelves inside the tall windows displayed *Cate's Cookery* preserves and savories in crystal containers etched with the delicate intertwined double CC of her logo. There stood slender bottles of her vinegars in every color and flavor, from lightest raspberry to deepest darkest balsamic, and jars of glistening English marmalade threaded with translucent slivers of bitter Seville orange and lemon rind. Deep red tomato chutney dotted with golden flecks of apples, onions and carrots shared space with glowing ginger pears suspended in thick syrups. Pink strawberry jam and deep plum preserves completed the edible still life.

Cate's state-of-the-art kitchen took up one entire side of the room and was equipped with gleaming stainless steel refrigerators, ovens, freezers, twin dishwashers and triple sinks.

The Diet

A glass-fronted pantry displayed neatly labeled canisters of sugars, flours, dried and candied fruits and other staples.

Copper-bottom pots, fish steamers, skeins of peppers and garlic braids hung from a suspended pot rack. White glazed canisters stuffed with whisks, wooden spoons, spatulas and ladles sat on the counters.

An old refectory table, stripped to bare wood and scrubbed and sweetened with lemon bleach, held a row of fat, unscented candles. Cate had one rule—no artificial smells. *The Cookery* was scented only with soft green herbs, fresh loam from the kitchen garden and the rich fragrances escaping from bubbling pots and baking ovens.

A clock chimed softly. Cate roused herself. It was time to get ready.

Her first cooking class of the day would arrive soon, and Sam was late again. Cate would have to act as organizer, teacher and her own assistant. She suppressed a wave of irritation. She felt too good and not even Sam's lack of responsibility would annoy her today.

With a final look around her beautiful *Cookery,* she stepped into the pantry to collect the ingredients she would need for her lesson. She had decided the class would make Cate's Celebration Cake.

As she piled the blocks of imported chocolate, bars of butter, bowls of brown eggs and baskets of raspberries and limes on the counter, she couldn't have imagined that she was assembling the end of her perfect life.

Chapter 16

"We must be about to make something really special," said Sue, a cheerful blonde whose cooking was like her dimple, surprising and always fun. "Just look at all this stuff," she exclaimed as she poked through the piles of ingredients, pans and whisks neatly lined up on the cooking counter.

"Doesn't Cate look terrific?" whispered Bette, a gaunt Connecticut matron who sandwiched *Cate's Cookery* classes between her bridge club and her dog shows.

"She always looks wonderful," answered Patricia in her small, quiet voice, eager never to disagree, always to please.

"What's all this? What are we making today, Cate?" asked Robbie, the only male member of the class. He was the son of Robert Bricosse, owner of *La Petite Pomme*, the best French restaurant in upstate New York. Rumor had it that Robbie was going to open his own place soon and was brushing up on his culinary skills.

"Today," replied Cate, stepping behind the counter and tying the stiff white chef's apron tightly around her

The Diet

waist, "I do have a surprise for you. We're going to make my Celebration Cake."

There was an excited buzz from her students. Cate had never before parted with the recipe. It was her most splendid creation and, up to now, a secret.

"What's the occasion?" asked the outspoken Sue "It must be something really special."

Cate's only answer was a smile.

For the next thirty minutes, they all happily sifted flour and baking powder, creamed sweet butter and added thin streams of fine sugar to the batter.

Then Cate divided her class into two groups, one to prepare the apricot preserves and the other the apricot custard for the filling between the cake layers.

"How did you ever come up with this incredible creation? " asked Bette, licking a smear of butter off her hand.

"I got the recipe from a wonderful lady who was my foster mother for a short time."

The class exchanged looks. This was indeed a special day. Cate rarely shared any of her private life. She always focused on the lesson or on her students. She had a way with people just as she had a way with food.

"She told me," Cate continued, oblivious of the heightened interest she had created, "that it had come from her mother who got it from a great, great, great…" Cate laughed. "That's probably too many greats, but anyway a great aunt who was the assistant pastry cook in the royal court of Czar Nicolas. She brought it to America with her right after the Russian revolution."

After giving the short history of the magnificent cake, she stepped over to the stove where Patricia was struggling with a double boiler.

"I just can't seem to get the right consistency," she said apologetically.

"It's fine," said Cate, giving the custard a brisk stir with a clean long-handled wooden spoon. "Did you remember the mashed apricots? The lemon juice and the lemon zest? The sugar, flour and the beaten egg yolks?"

Patricia nodded.

"Good, I turn over the spoon to you," said Cate with a flourish and slight bow. "Just remember to keep stirring until the custard gets thick. And be patient."

The door to *The Cookery* opened and slammed shut. The class turned, distracted, as Gena Rice rushed down the center of the space, dropping coat, briefcase, portfolio and Prada tote along the way.

"Sorry I'm late," she said, throwing her slim black jacket over the back of a chair, pushing up the stiff French cuffs of her custom shirt and scrubbing her hands at one of the kitchen sinks. Then she dried her hands on a kitchen towel that had been wrapped around a steaming bowl of freshly-cooked apricot purée.

"I couldn't get out of the office. Then traffic was brutal. And the train was late—what else is new?"

Her excuses were delivered in a frantic, breathless voice. It always seemed to Cate that Gena never inhaled.

The Diet

Everything about her reminded Cate of a New York City cab—always loud, always fast, always late.

She was Cate's newest student and a bit of mystery. She left the section describing her occupation blank when filling out *The Cookery* information sheet and refused to be drawn into any personal admissions.

Even though she had started coming to class just a few weeks ago, she had insisted on being placed in the advanced class.

At first the others closed ranks and shut her out, but Gena soon won them over.

She was so outrageous, from her dark eyes, rimmed with thick fake lashes, to her white platinum hair, short and spiked with gel, to her oversized silver and turquoise jewelry. Gena was an original. She had a passion for food. She loved it and it loved her back.

"Okay everyone, let's get back to work," said Cate.

Chapter 17

Class was over. The cake lesson had been a huge success. Cate's cash register rang with sales of spring-form pans, double boilers and whisks, sacks of dried apricots and hand-cut slabs of Belgian chocolate.

With every package she offered some last-minute advice to each of her students.

"Remember," she told Sue, who was struggling with two brimming shopping bags, "no shortcuts. Don't melt chocolate in the microwave. Use a double boiler."

"Bette, don't forget your apricot preserve recipe. Your cake will taste much better and your friends will be so impressed if you tell them you made your own fillings."

"Remember what Thomas Wolfe said," she whispered to Pat, the hesitant cook who took lessons to please her demanding husband. " 'There is no sight on earth more appealing that the sight of a woman making dinner for someone she loves.' And if that doesn't melt his heart," Cate added with a hug, "hang a mirror over the stove and cook to please yourself."

The Diet

When the last sale was rung up and the last package wrapped, Cate suddenly realized just how hot and tired she was.

Sam had never shown up to help and now Cate was faced with the devastation that only a class full of enthusiastic and hungry cooks can leave behind.

The counters, littered with bowls, whisks and cake pans were sticky with smears of chocolate, spilled egg yolk and bits of butter. The three sinks were piled with pots, cutlery and assorted bowls. Both dishwashers gaped open, waiting to be filled with tasting plates, cups, saucers and glasses. The table was strewn with crumbs.

All that remained of the first cake they baked was just one small slice, toppled over on its side and missing a layer.

But the second cake, the one she was taking home to Charles, stood untouched and glorious on its antique china pedestal. Six layers tall, covered in snow-white frosting, draped with ribbons of chocolate, it was encircled with rounds of golden apricots, red raspberries and delicate leaves made of candied lime peel. The crowning touch was a garden of edible flowers—delicate pink pansies, mauve violets and pure blue cornflowers.

Cate indulged herself for a moment and imagined Charles' pleasure, first at the dinner, then in the cake, and then at her news.

"Stop dreaming," she said aloud, giving herself a little mental shake. "The faster you start cleaning up, the faster you can get home."

With a soft sigh, she rolled up her sleeves and started to wipe down the counter when she was startled by a voice saying her name.

"Sorry, I didn't mean to make you jump," apologized Gena.

"That's okay. I thought everyone had left. What can I do for you?" asked Cate, her smile returning, fatigue forgotten.

"Actually, I would like to do something for you," said Gena.

Chapter 18

"I'm an executive editor at *Middleton & March*," announced Gena, naming one of the country's largest publishing conglomerates and in typical Gena fashion adding without inhaling, "I'd like to offer you a two hundred thousand dollar advance to write a book."

Cate opened her mouth to speak, but nothing came out.

"That's just for starters," Gena rushed on. "This is going to be a big book for us and for you. By the time we've marketed and promoted it, you could make a million dollars or more."

She started pulling stiff sheets of mounting board out of the black art portfolio, "We're going to call it *Cate's Cookery Cookbook.*"

She spoke with confidence, as if the book were already on the shelves. "It'll showcase your divine recipes—your preserves, those to-die-for quenelles, your berry vinegars, that decadent Bavarian cream you make, your rumaki and seviche. *Cate's Cookery Cookbook* will have it all, from your incredible baked artichokes to that amazing chocolate Zabaglione. We're even going to include your signature Celebration Cake."

"Why me?" asked Cate, recovering her voice.

"Because we believe there's a massive untapped market out there for a new kind of cookbook and a new kind of cook…"

Gena picked up her ringing cell phone. "I'm in a meeting," she said, and continued as if she hadn't been interrupted. "…someone who can show readers what it's like to have a love affair with food, someone who can turn the kitchen into the sexiest room in the house, someone who can whip up real butter, cream and eggs and still look beautiful and slender. You do that, Cate. You're perfect."

"I don't know what to say,"

"Wait till you hear the rest, then just say yes."

"You mean there's more?" Cate was already dazzled.

"It gets better," promised Gena. " We checked out your local television segments and we love you on camera…"

Cate was about to interrupt, but Gena didn't give her a chance.

She held up her hand and went on, "…so our media division is going to tie the book into your very own national cooking show."

Cate sat down, stunned.

But it was Gena's next words that made her heart stop and her hands grip the edge of the counter.

The Diet

"Here's the best part," said Gena, as she lifted up one of the large art boards and turned it to face Cate. "We're putting skinny you on the cover!"

Chapter 19

Cate stared at the huge blow-up of the proposed cover. There she was, full length in the center of what was an artist's rendering of *The Cookery*.

The classic chef's apron, with its long strings doubled across her narrow waist and tied in the front, accentuated her slimness.

She couldn't catch her breath.

"Are you all right?" Gena inhaled long enough to notice Cate had gone completely white. "Let me get you a glass of water."

"How can I be on the cover of a book?" Cate panicked privately as she tried to come to grips with the news and what it meant. "I'm going to have a baby. I'm going to be lucky if I can even tie an apron all the way around my waist much less be a cover girl. I'm going to be huge."

Fighting rising nausea and panic, she couldn't catch her breath. "What am I going to do?" Her thoughts spun round and round, out of control.

"Is it possible after all this struggle that it happens this fast?" she wondered to herself. "Is it possible that in one moment a person walks into your life and hands you everything you ever wanted, everything you ever worked for, just like that?"

She considered the future Gena had just offered like some modern fairy godmother.

"A guaranteed future. Recognition. Fame. Money. Financial security for all of us."

Cate knew how Cinderella must have felt.

"But Cinderella wasn't pregnant," she reminded herself. "I am."

Chapter 20

"Do you want lemon in your water?" asked Gena from behind the counter.

"Yes please," answered Cate, stalling for time to get her emotions under control and decide what do to.

"Wonderful Gena with her magic publishing wand doesn't know I'm pregnant. Should I tell her? Do I *have* to tell her? And what about the doctor? He said I had to take it easy. I don't think this is exactly what he meant."

Even now, Cate could feel the tension building in her. A nervous giggle escaped her lips.

Gena took it for excitement. "I'll be there in a sec." Her cell phone shrilled again and Cate listened as Gena talked and sliced at the same time.

Cate gripped the edge of the counter even harder until her nails were blanched of color.

"Could life be so cruel?" Suddenly she was uncharacteristically angry.

"How could life give me the most precious gift of all, the gift I prayed and prayed for—a child—and on the same day hand me this other extraordinary gift of fame

The Diet

and real security? How can I make a choice? A baby or a book?"

"Here's your water," said Gena handing the cold, brimming glass to Cate.

Cate suddenly came to her senses, her decision made. There was no choice.

"Listen Gena," Cate began to turn down the book and explain about the baby, but her throat was dry and her lips parched, and she paused to take a sip of water.

That slight pause was enough for Gena. She jumped right back into the monologue she had interrupted to pour the water. "The publication date is set for Christmas."

"Christmas," echoed Cate weakly.

"Next Christmas," laughed Gena. "Publishing doesn't work that fast. That's about fourteen months from now. That should give you lots of time to select the recipes. It'll give us time to edit and design the book, plan the television show, and get the pre-launch publicity started."

"And the cover?" asked Cate.

"We'll probably schedule the photo shoot for the cover around the end of July or beginning of August of next year."

Cate did the math, counting off the months faster than she had ever counted before. This was the beginning of October. The baby was due in June. She had a whole month, maybe even six weeks after the baby was born, to get back into shape for the cover photo.

The Diet

She was going to be fine. There was to be no choice after all. Cate could have her baby *and* her book. She could now tell Gena about the pregnancy.

"You look better. You've got your color back," said Gena. "Got to run. I'll call you in a couple of days and set up a meeting in New York to go over everything and meet everyone."

"Listen Gena," Cate began, relieved and eager to break the news about the baby, "before you go I'd just like to tell you…"

"Save it for next week," Gena answered, as her cell phone rang again.

Moments later, gathering up her briefcase, portfolio and shopping bag and swinging her designer tote, over her shoulder Gena gave Cate a quick peck on the cheek. A final *ciao* and Gena was gone.

Cate sat for a few minutes, sipping her water. Then she slid off the stool and stepped back around the counter to the piles of dirty dishes. Needing something calming and ordinary to do, she filled the sinks with hot soapy water.

While her hands scrubbed away at the encrusted pots and sticky pans, Cate's mind went over the incredible blessings of the day. She felt overwhelmingly, supremely happy. Life was good—perfect, in fact.

What Cate didn't realize was that while life could bestow blessings in abundance, it could just as easily snatch them all away.

Chapter 21

It was after eleven o'clock and Charles wasn't home. Cate went from frantic to furious every five minutes.

The candles she lit at seven o'clock had melted down to stubs. The fettuccini was a gluey paste. The crusty bread dried out and the veal had turned to rubber. The ice in the silver champagne bucket had melted back to water hours ago and sweated through her best antique linen and lace tablecloth. Even her ginger ale had gone flat. Her celebration dinner was ruined.

She had just decided to start calling his partners when she heard his key in the lock and the familiar Charles sounds: his briefcase toppling over on the hardwood floor, the closet door opening, the clank of a wooden hanger and at last his footsteps coming down the hall.

Then she saw him.

His normally neat reddish hair was messed as if he had run his hands through it repeatedly. His gray eyes were bloodshot and smudged with fatigue. His mouth was set in a grim line. The top button of his shirt was undone, and his shirt collar was stained with sweat. His loosened tie hung crooked. He looked exhausted and something more. He looked afraid.

Normally Cate, seeing him this way, would have rushed over, held him in her arms and soothed him with gentle whispers.

But this hadn't been a normal day. Cate was too full of her own emotions and her own news. She picked up a glass of lukewarm Champagne and a gaily-wrapped package and handed both to him.

"Go ahead," she urged, her voice filled with excitement, her anger at his unexplained lateness disappearing now that he was safely home. "Open it."

Charles set down the glass with exaggerated slowness and pulled off the wrapping paper to reveal the book *What To Expect When You're Expecting*. Momentarily confused, he stared at the title and then at her glowing face. Then, comprehension dawned.

But Cate, watching carefully for that first sign of delight, was bitterly disappointed. What she saw was not joy, but shock, then disbelief, then nothing. Charles' face had shut down.

Before she could react, the front door slammed, and seconds later Sam rushed into the room, dropping her keys on the dining room table.

"I've got the most fantastic news," she blurted out, completely ignoring the rigid figures of Cate and Charles. "You'll never guess." Not waiting for them to try, she went on, "I'm in love and this is the best part, I'm going to be on television."

Cate looked at Charles and then at Sam and burst into tears.

She sobbed with rage, fatigue and disappointment. They had robbed her of the pleasure of sharing, of telling them about the baby and about the book. Most of all, they had robbed her of the spotlight.

She was suddenly supremely tired of being the constant older, wiser sister and the ever-patient and supporting wife.

Today of all days she wanted to be their center of attention. Now her perfect day was spoiled.

Chapter 22

Cate's outburst immediately brought Sam to her side.

"What's wrong?" she asked, hugging Cate awkwardly. "I thought you'd be excited for me."

"Sam," interrupted Charles, turning the book he was holding around so that Sam could see the cover. "I think Cate has news of her own."

"Oh Cate, a baby! I'm going to be an aunt!" Sam jumped up, poured herself a glass of Champagne, lifted it in a toast and drank most of it down.

Cate's thoughts were dark. "All she can think of is that she's going to be an aunt. What about me? I'm going to be a mother."

Cate surprised herself. She had devoted her entire life to Sam and never had a single thought like the one that had just crossed her mind.

Sam, trying to get Cate to smile, raised her glass in a second toast. "To our family," she said, giving Charles a sharp poke.

The Diet

"To our family," he repeated, picking up and raising his own glass.

Suddenly Cate's anger and disappointment dissolved like threads of cotton candy on the tip of a warm tongue, and she was flooded with an intense love for them both.

Raising her glass of ginger ale, she stepped into the circle and echoed, "To our family."

Chapter 23

With the fragile mood restored, Cate slipped into her role of big sister once again.

She focused on Sam and set aside her own news about the book and especially the national television show she had been offered.

"Now what's this about falling in love? And what about a television show? Tell me everything."

Sam was wild with excitement as she told them about the amazing Dr. Paul Glazer, M.D., PhD., she had just met and fallen in love with.

"He's brilliant. He's not even forty yet and has his own pharmaceutical company, can you imagine? And get this; he has developed a new diet pill. And he wants me to be his spokesperson on television."

Cate and Charles exchanged a marital glance.

In that exchange was their lifetime of experience with Sam.

Restless and flighty, she threw her petite one hundred pound body into one weight-loss idea after another. And then, a few months later, bored and restless she would move on to something else.

Completely unreliable, she never worried about money or men or the future.

She had charm and was beautiful, with fine blonde hair that shone around her shoulders. Her skin was delicate, so transparent you could see the faint blue veins throbbing in her temple. Her eyes were pale pastel blue fringed with dark lashes and crowned by dark eyebrows, a striking combination.

Model thin, she loved to wear slim Capri pants and crisp white shirts tied at the midriff and high-heeled strappy sandals. She always wore four rings, simple circles of gold, one on each ring finger and one on each index finger.

Sam was passionate about her clothes, her looks and her figure.

"But you don't know anything about television and what about your classes at the Culinary Institute," asked Cate, trying hard not to rain on Sam's parade but also trying to be realistic.

"What's to know?' shrugged Sam.

Cate tried again to bring her wild sister back to earth.

"Sam, you've never taken a diet pill in your life. You never had to. How can you be a spokesperson for a product you've never used?"

Turning away for a moment to refill her glass, Cate failed to see the guilty look that crossed Sam's face. If she

The Diet

had, she might have raised more objections and fought harder to keep Sam from plunging into yet another mad scheme. But Cate didn't see the clues in Sam's face and when she turned back, Sam was smiling and refilling her own glass and topping up Charles'.

"It's just another one of her crackpot diets," Charles teased. "Remember those sunglasses she wore for months that were supposed to project a diet message directly into her eyeballs?"

"I remember the time she gave me that bar of diet soap that was supposed to flush away fat with every shower," added Cate.

"Or those slippers she made me wear," laughed Charles, "the ones that had magnets in them and fat was supposed to travel down and get trapped in your feet. All they ever did was give me sore feet."

"Go ahead and laugh," said Sam, taking the teasing with her usual good nature. "But these diet pills are the real thing, and when I make millions I'm going to buy my niece or nephew an entire toy store. But first, what do you have to eat? I'm starving."

"I'm afraid dinner's ruined," said Cate, avoiding Charles eyes.

"The cake isn't," said Sam noticing the lavish dessert on the dining room sideboard. "Cake and Champagne. Who could ask for a better celebration?"

Nodding her agreement, Cate went over to the sideboard, picked up the cake knife, and cut a slice for Sam and another for Charles.

The Diet

"What about you?" he asked.

Cate shook her head. She loved to cook. She loved the feel of food in her hands. She loved the warm, rich smells of a kitchen. But Cate herself was afraid to indulge. She ate very little and settled just for tiny little tastes of what she made.

For the third time that day, her mother came into her mind, her mother who had left her with two such contradictory gifts, the love of cooking, and the fear of food.

The Diet

Chapter 24

Charles slammed his plate so hard on the sideboard that she jumped.

"I'm sick of watching you cook and fix and prepare food you never eat," he burst out, his bad mood returning. "Look at Sam. She eats whatever she wants and she never gains an ounce. For crying out loud, you both share the same genes. Why are you always so afraid of getting fat?"

"Maybe Charles was right," she rationalized. "Sam ate anything and everything and burned it off in seconds and always stayed a perfect size four. After all, they did share the same genes."

To keep the peace and placate Charles she said, "You're right. How can one piece hurt?" and cut herself a slice of the towering Celebration Cake.

"And one for the baby," Charles demanded. "Remember, you're eating for two now."

Cate added a second slice to the first.

Slowly, while Charles watched, she brought the first forkful to her lips. As its sweetness melted on her

The Diet

tongue she had a flashback of her mother lying in a mess of cookie crumbs and spilled ice cream.

She forced the image away and swallowed. But the damage was done. What Cate forgot under the onslaught of Charles' outburst and remembered in the taste of the cake was that she also shared her mother's genes.

Chapter 25

The next morning Cate was on her knees clutching the toilet bowl. Her only comfort was the fact that none of the cake calories she had consumed the previous night could possibly survive this attack of morning sickness.

Finally the spasms stopped. She ventured shakily into the bedroom and was sitting exhausted on the edge of the bed when the phone rang.

"Hello," she managed, nearly dropping the receiver.

"Cate? Dr. Selig here. I just got your test results back and I'd like to see you right away. Can you come in first thing Monday morning?"

Her stomach heaved, and she fought down a fresh wave of nausea.

"What's wrong? Is it the baby?"

"It's not the baby," said Dr. Selig in that calm voice used by doctors and airline pilots. "It's you, Cate. You're what we call a high-risk pregnancy."

"What do you mean?"

The Diet

"I'll explain in detail when I see you. In the meantime, I want you to take it easy and don't worry. Get plenty of rest. Stay off your feet as much as possible. I don't want to have to keep you in bed for the whole term. Do as I say, and everything will be just fine." With that he was gone.

"How can I take it easy?" she worried. "There's the book to write and my television segments to tape and the weekly column at *The Record*. Then there's *The Cookery* and all the cooking classes. And that doesn't even count running the house and all the errands. How am I supposed to stay off my feet?"

Still a little wobbly, she went downstairs to the kitchen. She opened the fridge and was about to reach for a bottle of chilled water when she saw the leftover Celebration Cake.

Suddenly, she was ravenous.

She reached into the cutlery drawer for a fork and speared a piece of the cake. Its cool sweetness soothed her.

She felt better.

The next piece made her feel better still.

Ten minutes later, energized by the sugar rush, she had her entire pregnancy organized.

Sam would just have to settle down and run *The Cookery*. She would drop her television segments and resign *The Record*. Josh would have to find someone else to write a food column.

The Diet

Then she would be free to stay home, just like Dr. Selig wanted, rest, relax and test recipes for her book.

She took another bite of cake to celebrate her organizational skills and heard a car door slam.

Glancing out the window she saw Charles.

"He must have forgotten something," she imagined. "Too bad he had to drive all the way back from the office. I hope he's in a better mood than he was last night."

She closed the fridge and tossed her fork into the sink. She would greet Charles with a big smile and an even bigger hug.

She felt wonderful.

What she didn't realize was that in the ten minutes it had taken to convince herself that everything was under control and would be just fine, she had eaten almost half the remaining cake.

The Diet

Chapter 26

"Hi Charles, did you forget something?" Cate called out.

Silence was the only response she got.

Her resolve to greet him with a smile dissolved into irritation by his continued moodiness.

She called out again. "Did you forget something?"

"No, I didn't forget anything," he snapped, walking into the kitchen and dropping his briefcase in the middle of the floor. Then he went to the cupboard where they kept their liquor and poured himself a generous Scotch.

"What's wrong?"

Charles just stood at the sink and downed his drink.

"What's happened? Why are you drinking at ten o'clock in the morning? Talk to me, Charles."

"You want to know what happened?" he asked bitterly, "it's over, that's what's happened. It's finished." He poured himself a second large Scotch.

"What's over?"

"The company, my job, everything. The place was padlocked when I drove up this morning, and there was a marshal's seal across the doors."

"But Charles, everything was fine yesterday," Cate said, confused.

Then she remembered how late he was coming home and how moody and irritable he had been. She should have known that something was very wrong. She should have paid more attention to him.

"Didn't you have a hint, an idea? How could this happen so suddenly? How could you not know?"

"The money wasn't my job. I was the designer, remember?" he said sarcastically. "I didn't know what went on in accounting or sales. I had partners who took care of that end. Well, they took care of it all right."

With that he hurled his empty glass into the sink.

"Bill suspected something last night. But even he didn't think it would be this bad."

Cate put her arms around him and rested her cheek against the rough fiber of his woolen coat. They stood like that for a few minutes, Cate holding him tight and whispering, "It's going to be okay."

"It's not going to be okay."

Charles pulled away from her.

"How can it be okay? By the time this mess gets sorted out it could cost us all our savings. How are we going to manage? Who knows how long it'll be before I can get another job. And now with the baby and everything…"

The Diet

He choked off a sob and turned his face away.

"Listen Charles, it really is going to be okay. We've got lots of money, more than we've ever had in our lives."

Cate took him by the hand, led him gently to the kitchen table, sat him down and for the next hour told him all about Gena, *Middleton & March*, and the book contract with its two hundred thousand dollar advance.

What she didn't tell him was the doctor's warning. She left that out.

"You can have the money, Charles. You don't have to look for a job. You can start your own company now or maybe even buy one. See, everything's working out."

Cate finished, satisfied that she could look after him again. "Now, how about some breakfast?"

She went to the fridge and pulled out the remains of their Celebration Cake.

"You know, "she grinned at him, "this could be the best thing that ever happened to us. Anyway, how bad can things be? We're eating cake for breakfast."

And so Cate ate her second cake breakfast of the day.

Chapter 27

The curtains were closed against the early afternoon sun. Charles was asleep. They had finished the cake in bed and then made love the way they had when they were first married.

Cate leaned on one elbow and watched the slow, steady rise and fall of his chest. With the tip of her finger, she lifted a small crumb that was caught in the corner of his mouth and brought it to her own lips. Then she curled her body against his and closed her eyes.

Her dreams during that long afternoon sleep were of babies and of books.

They were to be the last sweet dreams Cate would have for a long time.

Chapter 28

"Everybody, I'd like you to meet Cate, of *Cate's Cookery*, soon to be Cate of *The Cookery Cookbook* and *The Cooking with Cate Show!*" said Gena, introducing Cate enthusiastically to the sea of smiling and expectant faces around the long conference table.

Every department was represented: editorial, sales, publicity, rights and some others Cate didn't have a chance to identify. That was just on the publishing side.

Then there was the contingent from the media division: two producers, a researcher, a director and three writers.

"Well, I'll just leave you all to get acquainted," announced Gena, turning to leave and with a wave added, "I'll be back."

Cate was disappointed. She had hoped to have a quiet word with Gena to tell her about the baby, but so far she hadn't had the opportunity.

Undaunted, Cate unpacked two big hampers filled with some of her most tempting recipes and passed the containers down the length of the table.

The Diet

There were small dishes to sample: a fried eggplant salad with Feta cheese and fresh basil and a gingered noodle salad garnished with slivers of fresh tuna. There was a couscous salad and crisp prawns with blue cheese curled into leaves of lettuce and a peppered beef and cucumber salad with white wine vinegar and sesame oil.

She brought steamed pork buns, lacy potato cakes with smoked salmon, miniature pizzas plump with tomatoes, olives and studded with fresh rosemary, sliced steak on rounds of black bread topped with roasted garlic paste, breaded risotto cakes and a coarse pâté seasoned with cognac and presented with freshly-baked baguettes.

Then she displayed the desserts. There were flaky pastries filled with hazelnut cream, white chocolate tarts, chilled pears poached in coconut milk, slices of pineapple cake finished with toasted pecans as well as ladyfingers, macaroons and meringues.

They ate with relish, complimenting her on every dish.

Jim Cleary, the CFO, interrupted his number crunching to sample one of Cate's white chocolate tarts and Fred Leech, the publisher, came in to meet her and welcome her to the *Middleton & March* family, and left with a plate to take back to his office.

Finally, all the questions had been asked and answered. All the hands had been shaken. All the dishes were empty.

They loved her; each one assured her with a New York peck on her cheek, as they left the conference room.

The Diet

Cate was alone with the mess. And still no Gena.

"Hi, I'm Chip. Gena asked me to give you a hand," said a young man who came into the room and started to pile the containers back into Cate's hamper.

"Where is Gena?" Cate asked. "I have to talk to her for a few minutes."

"On her way to the airport by now. She's going on a major scouting trip, looking for new talent all over Europe."

"Europe," said Cate, stunned. "When will she be back?"

"I don't really know, they don't tell me much," he replied. "Wish I could go."

Cate had lost her chance to tell Gena about the baby.

Chapter 29

The weeks and months passed.

Cate signed her contract, cashed the first half of her six-figure advance and gave more than half the money to Charles.

First he tried to buy one company, then another, but something always went wrong. Failure followed failure. He spent weeks looking, and just as he found something, the deal went sour on him.

Then he tried to start his own business, but that effort stalled when the bank refused to extend a business loan to him to supplement Cate's funding.

He lacked basic financial skills, and his natural suspicion of anything new made it hard for him to trust or even understand experts. Frustrated and feeling out of his depth, he would come home fuming at the lawyer and accountant who tried to help him set up basic systems and procedures.

Charles saw himself as an independent success, but resented the enormous personal effort he was expected to invest.

The Diet

Every day he became more discouraged and sullen. Jealous of Cate's success and the constant enthusiastic phone calls, memos and overnight packages from her publisher in New York, he withdrew from her.

Abandoned, physically and emotionally by Charles, Cate was on her own in their marriage.

Recalling the comfort in those cool mouthfuls of Celebration Cake, Cate turned more and more to the solace of sugar and gained over eight pounds in the three weeks before Halloween. She added another twelve by Thanksgiving.

Chapter 30

Sam also turned out to be no help.

She spent more and more time with her new love the diet doctor and less and less time taking classes at the Institute or helping Cate at *The Cookery*.

Finally, weeping in Cate's arms, she confessed that she hated *The Cookery* and cooking and everything to do with food. She pleaded with Cate to give her the money to go to California with her doctor. He had offered to let her buy a small piece of his company. It was the chance of a lifetime. She would be his partner. She could create something of her very own, something that she could become successful at without Cate. She would be a grown-up. She begged Cate for the money that would make her independent.

Cate, never able to refuse her baby sister anything, gave her the rest of the money she had set aside from her advance.

Sam flew to Los Angeles with her diet doctor and left Cate to run *The Cookery* alone.

The Diet

Day after day, Cate ran *The Cookery*. She taught. She cooked. She cleaned up. And she ate.

It was the season for food. *The Cookery* was filled to overflowing with holiday goodies. Classes, packed with old students and new, learned how to shape intricately iced gingerbread into houses and sleds, how to press buttery shortbread into carved wooden baking molds and how to take a pound each of butter, flour, sugar and eggs and turn it into a tall stately pound cake.

She taught the art of stuffing a plump Dickens goose, then rendering the rich fragrant fat and turning it into casseroles of confit.

She showed them how to make holiday butters and traditional mincemeat pies, puddings and even edible tree ornaments.

Cate went from small tastes to full portions of everything her classes cooked. Then, after the doors were locked and she was alone, she ate the leftovers, too.

By Christmas Day, Cate was another fourteen pounds heavier.

Chapter 31

But as difficult as her days were, her nights were even harder because they belonged to *Middleton & March*. Bought and paid for, Cate had a contract that bound her to produce.

And so she did. She developed, cooked, tested and ate the recipes for her book. When she wasn't eating "book" samples, she was reviewing and revising scripts for her new national cooking show, working up TV-friendly recipes and eating those as well.

Cate worked and ate until well past midnight seven days a week.

The grueling days and lonely nights ground away at her strength. She was stressed and pressured by constant demands and deadlines and worries.

Charles, cracking under his own inability to build a business, stayed away more and more, getting home later and later.

On those rare nights he stayed home, Charles locked himself in their small home office, surfed the net and drank Scotch until the early hours.

They hadn't sat down to a meal together in weeks. Each one ate alone.

Cate also worried about Sam. She began to second-guess her decision to give Sam the money to go to L.A. She was afraid for Sam and, while she couldn't put her finger on exactly why, she felt a growing distrust of the diet doctor.

With every cell in her body quivering from fatigue and with her mind racing from one problem to the other, Cate got little sleep.

Despite her growing fatigue, she got up and did it all over again the next morning.

When she ran out of classes and recipes of her own, she took shortcuts to feed her tired body the instant energy of simple carbs it craved to keep going.

At first she began to snack on candy bars. Then she began to pull into the drive-though on her way home for a big sloppy fast-food burger in a bag. Dinner was more often than not a huge bowl of cold cereal drowned in sugar to help her get through the rest of the long night.

All these foods soothed her frazzled nerves, brought her momentary comfort and, most of all, gave her the energy she so desperately needed to keep going. But all these foods sent her weight climbing steadily upwards.

Chapter 32

"Cate, you're gaining too much weight," Dr. Selig warned her at the end of October, at the end of November and again before Christmas. After each visit he gave her pamphlets on pre-natal diets.

Cate dutifully took each one, but when she climbed back into the car, and let out the seat belt even further to accommodate her growing bulk, she shoved the new pamphlets into the glove compartment with all the others.

But it wasn't only her weight that Dr. Selig was unhappy with. He lectured her on her blood pressure, her lack of rest, her water retention and her frequent infections.

Unable to cope with his mounting displeasure, she skipped an appointment, then a second and then a third, which was her sonogram appointment.

By Valentine's Day, Cate hadn't been to the doctor in several weeks, and had gained over fifty pounds.

Through all those long months she kept telling herself to hold on a little longer.

The Diet

She just needed a little more time until Charles got a business started, until Sam grew bored with her diet doctor and came home to help at *The Cookery*, until she finished the book for *Middleton & March*, until the baby was born. She would lose weight. She would stop eating. Everything would go back to normal.

All she needed was just a little more time.

Then, one spring afternoon, Dr. Selig's warnings came true and Cate ran out of time.

Chapter 33

It was an early spring afternoon. Cate had just been to the post office to send out the completed manuscript to *Middleton & March* and had pulled into the market. She was loading the last of a dozen grocery bags for her five o'clock cooking class into the back of her car when she felt a sharp pain in her side so severe she gasped and doubled over.

"Are you all right?" a concerned voice asked. It was Josh. He lifted the heavy bag out of her arms.

"Fine. Just a little tired," gasped Cate, straightening up slowly and bracing herself against another stab of pain.

"What you need is a cup of tea," said Josh.

"No thank you. I'm fine," she protested. "I've got too much to do. I don't really have the time."

Cate was ashamed. She hadn't talked to Josh in months. She hadn't even tried to contact him since that day she walked into his office, told him about the book deal and quit her job as his food columnist.

She had even stopped reading *The Record*.

The Diet

He had been gracious, but she saw the look of disappointment in his eyes that she would drop him so quickly when a better offer came along. But he never said a word. He didn't have to.

The last thing she wanted was to sit across a table from him, make small talk and feel guilty.

"Honestly, I've got a new class starting in a couple of hours," she protested again.

But Josh was already leading her to the small café across the street.

"My mother lived through five years of war in London, and bombs or no bombs she maintained there was always time for tea."

Cate gave up and let herself be led into the café and settled at a window table. She let Josh select the herbal tea and made no protest when he added buttery scones, raspberry jam and Devonshire cream so thick a spoon could stand upright in it.

"It feels good to be looked after for a change, fussed over, if only for a little while," Cate thought.

Their tea arrived and they sat together sipping. Josh talked to her quietly about simple things—a hiking trip he was planning in the mountains, the upcoming town elections, the weather.

He didn't mention *The Record* or that he hadn't replaced either her columns or her. He didn't mention how much he missed her.

Cate forgot how tired she was and found she was enjoying herself. She sipped her tea, listened, and recalled how much he had meant to her. Remembering, she realized how much she missed his gentle ways, his inner strength and his sure touch.

While he talked, Josh observed her and was shocked by the changes.

Her once shining hair was lifeless. Her smooth skin had grown rough and blemished. Her sparkling eyes were dull and rimmed with red, their delicate skin smudged with dark circles of fatigue.

But most of all he was shocked by her size.

This was no ordinary weight gain from a baby.

She was big all over. Her neck, arms and calves had thickened. Her ankles were swollen and so were her fingers. Her face was puffy. He could see the rolls of flesh under her thin cotton maternity shirt where the straps of her bra dug into the fatty skin.

Cate, laughing at something he said, suddenly excused herself.

She started to rise and in an instant Josh was around the back of her chair, pulling it out and helping her up.

He saw the fresh blood stain on the seat at the same instant that Cate cried out, clutched her side and collapsed to the floor.

The Diet

Chapter 34

"Cate. Open your eyes," a voice insisted. "Wake up now and open your eyes."

She felt someone lift her wrist and then cool firm fingers on her pulse. "She's coming around now, Doctor."

"And here she is," said a deeper voice she recognized. "Welcome back, Cate."

As she struggled to open her eyes, she saw the blurry face of Dr. Selig swimming in and out of focus.

"Don't try to talk yet," Dr. Selig said, "just lie still and listen. You're in the hospital. Josh Cody brought you in. Do you remember?"

She did. She remembered laughing, then a sharp pain and a warm wetness between her legs. Then nothing.

When she opened her eyes again everything was in focus.

She looked around slowly, still a little light-headed, and saw the monitors around her bed blinking with red and green and blue lights, the aluminum stand hung with bags of colored liquid and the IV lines running down into her arms.

The Diet

"The baby?" she cried. "Is the baby all right?"

"The baby is in our neonatal intensive care unit," said Dr. Selig carefully as he picked up her hand and held it gently. "Right now it's stable, but I won't kid you. Your baby isn't out of danger yet."

"I want to see my baby. Please. Let me see my baby," Cate struggled to get up but Dr. Selig held tight to her hand, and the cool fingers of the nurse gently but firmly forced her back down on the bed.

Cate fell back exhausted.

"Is it a girl or a boy?" she asked faintly.

"It's a beautiful girl," Dr. Selig said.

"We decided her name would be Charlie," Cate told them. Then she asked, "Where is Charles?"

Dr. Selig and the nurse looked at each other above her head.

"He's coming. He's on his way. Don't worry."

Charles had made it only as far as the hospital coffee shop. He had been sitting there for hours, his head in his hands, unable to cope with this new crisis in his life.

"Cate, you need to be very, very strong. Listen to me carefully now. There's more," Dr. Selig began while the nurse prepared a sedative.

"Cate, you had twins." He squeezed her hand tighter. "We couldn't save your son."

Chapter 35

For seven days Cate lay in her hospital bed.

Charles came up but left almost at once, unable to deal with his dead son, his premature and fragile daughter, or Cate. He didn't come up a second time.

Instead, Cate received a crisp, unsympathetic note from Mrs. Bea saying that Charles was with her and she was looking after him.

Dr. Selig took care of their dead son.

Baskets of fruit, bunches of flowers and cards arrived and filled her small room to overflowing. Josh came to visit every day. Sam flew back from Los Angeles and brought her tanned and athletic diet doctor with her for a quick visit. *The Cookery* students came.

It didn't matter. Cate couldn't stop crying.

Whenever Dr. Selig or one of the nurses suggested she visit the neonatal intensive care unit, she broke out in a sweat and soaked through her hospital gown and the bed sheets. Her pulse raced. She saw black spots before her eyes, and she fought for consciousness. Cate was in the grip of a violent post-partum depression.

The Diet

Chapter 36

Dr. Selig cut off all visits and prescribed a course of antidepressant medication.

She stopped crying then and started eating.

The only time she managed to leave her bed was late at night. She shuffled down the corridor in her gummy hospital socks to the vending machines in the waiting room and shuffled back with candy, pastries and chips that she hid in her dresser.

Late one night, lying in bed trying not to make a sound as she unwrapped a candy bar, she heard the duty nurses talking outside her door.

"Poor thing. I feel so sorry for her. Losing her baby like that and the other one still in intensive care."

"It's her own fault."

"What do you mean?"

"Didn't they teach you that in nursing school?"

"Teach me what?"

"That obesity is one of the triggers for premature

birth. Look at her chart. She gained over sixty pounds. No telling how much she would have gained if she had gone to full term. No need to feel sorry for her."

"Really?"

"Really. If she hadn't gained all that weight her baby would probably be alive, and the other one wouldn't be fighting for her life. If you ask me, she killed her baby with her fat."

Cate turned her face to the wall and wept, smearing tears and chocolate all over the pillow.

Chapter 37

After a week of medication and Dr. Selig's encouragement, Cate roused herself from the darkness in which she had spent the past days and went to see their baby for the first time.

That visit marked the beginning of a new routine for Cate.

Her life now revolved around the small plastic box that held her baby. She was completely oblivious to everything and everyone else. She spent every day and each night in the neonatal intensive care unit holding a solitary vigil, while her tiny daughter fought for her life.

She was consumed with guilt, her thoughts spinning with "if only's."

If only she hadn't been so caught up in the whole *Middleton & March* madness and had tried harder to tell Gena about her pregnancy.

If only she hadn't tried to finish the book.

If only she had been firm with Sam, demanding that she stay through the pregnancy to help.

The Diet

If only she had helped Charles more. She knew that deep down he was always so afraid and always needed someone to be there for him.

If only she had listened to the doctor.

If only she hadn't started on all that junk food.

If only she hadn't gotten so fat, her son might be alive and her daughter well and in her arms.

It always came back to that, to her fat. She couldn't get the voice of that nurse out of her head.

But now she couldn't stop. It was too late. And so Cate sat in the intensive care unit for weeks and rocked, and wept, and ate and grew fatter still.

Chapter 38

"Charles," Cate called, as she flung open the door of their house. "I've got great news. The baby is out of danger. She can come home soon. Did they tell you?" She rushed into the living room, the dining room, the small home office and the kitchen looking for him. All the rooms were empty.

"Are you up there, Charles?" she called as she went up the stairs, pulling herself along by the banister, to the bedroom.

"Charles, isn't that great? Everything is going to be fine. The baby is going to be fine. We're going to be fine. Charles, where are you?"

The last door she opened was to the nursery and she stopped in shock and disbelief.

The crib was gone and so were the antique rocker, the bassinette and even the merry-go-round lamp. All that was left was the pale yellow wallpaper, with the pink and blue butterflies, she had hung with such love. In the middle of the floor, where the rag rug used to be, stood Charles surrounded by boxes.

The Diet

"Charles, what's happening? Where are all the baby's things?"

"They're at Mrs. Bea's," Charles replied, "which is where I'm going and where I'm going to take the baby. She's going to look after us since you obviously can't."

"I don't understand. What are you saying?"

Instead of answering, he grabbed her arm, propelled her to their bedroom and shoved her in front of the full-length mirror.

"Look at yourself." His face contorted with childish fury. "If you had looked after the baby the way you were supposed to in the first place, the way I found out the doctor told you to, if you stayed on the diet he gave you, my son would still be alive. You killed my son, and I'm not going to let you destroy my daughter."

"You can't mean that!" Cate replied, stunned by his words. "That's not you talking Charles, that's Mrs. Bea."

Charles snorted in disgust. "Take a good look. You're not the beautiful Cate I married," he said and shoved her against the mirror.

As he stormed out of the room, he knocked over a picture. He bent down to pick it up, looked at it and flung it to floor at her feet. "You've turned into your mother."

The Diet

Chapter 39

Cate looked at her reflection in the mirror, and for the first time saw herself as Charles saw her.

The tops of her feet and her ankles were swollen with fat. Her calves had thickened. She was raw where her thighs rubbed together. Her belly hung in folds. She had no waist. Her breasts swung heavily. She put her hand up to her face. Where once it had been smooth and oval, it was now puffy and round. Her enormous eyes had shrunk into the fat cheeks, and the shadow of a double chin spoiled her once classic profile.

"Could this really be me?" she asked the mirror, seeing her mother in her own face and her own body.

She rushed into the bathroom and stepped on the scale. The needle swung and settled between the two hundred and four and two hundred and five pound mark.

She stepped off, as if the scale mat was covered in hot coals.

"That can't be right. Please," she sent up a silent plea, "don't let it be right."

The Diet

She stepped back on again. This time the needle stopped exactly on the mark. Two hundred and five pounds.

She had gained ninety pounds!

Walking back into the bedroom, she picked up the photo of her mother, the only one she had.

"Charles is right," she admitted to herself. "I'm exactly like my mother."

When she came downstairs, Charles was gone. She walked slowly through the empty rooms, alone and afraid.

To fill the emptiness, Cate opened the fridge and began to eat.

Chapter 40

Cate ate until she couldn't eat any more, but she couldn't eat away her emptiness or her fear.

Her whole life she had been in control. She had looked after everyone. Now when she needed them the most they had abandoned her.

She tried to organize her thoughts, tried to think clearly, but the antidepressant drugs and sugar rushing through her body clouded her thinking.

All she could do was feel an instinct, ancient and strong.

"I have to get my baby back. I have to get my husband back. I have to make us a family."

But how she would get Charles and the baby back defeated her. She couldn't form a single coherent plan.

"Oh, my God," she asked, "What am I going to do?"

The Diet

Chapter 41

Defeated, Cate opened the pantry, took out a big box of cereal, brought it over to the kitchen table, reached in and started to eat.

Then she saw the envelope.

It was one of the thick creamy white envelopes that Gena used. She tore open the flap and unfolded the single stiff sheet.

The first words she read—"loved your manuscript" were scrawled across the top in Gena's distinctive hand.

Cate hadn't thought about the manuscript, the book, Gena or *Middleton & March* since the day she collapsed.

It all seemed unreal, as if Gena, *Middleton & March* and even the book belonged to some other person living some other life.

Suddenly, her mind cleared. Her thoughts dropped into place. A calm came over her.

Her cry for help had been heard.

It was in the second paragraph.

The Diet

The letter said that the publishers were reviewing her manuscript and had booked the studio for the cover shoot. It would take place in New York in three months—in August—at which time *Middleton & March* would sign off on the whole project and present her with the other half of her advance.

She hadn't lost everything quite yet. She could still get it all back. They could all be the family she had dreamed of for so long. It wasn't impossible. The money was waiting for her—for them. All she had to do was lose ninety pounds in ninety days.

"How hard could that be?" Cate asked herself.

The Diet

Chapter 42

It was incredibly hard.

First she tried to lose on the most popular diet. Then she switched to the second most popular. Four weeks and four diets later she was stalled.

She lost something on each diet and then she gained it all back plus a few extra pounds.

She was always hungry. She suffered from mood swings so severe she thought she had split in two, Cate and her evil twin. Time and time again, no matter how much will power she exerted, intense cravings shook her, not letting go, until she satisfied them.

All she could think of was finding that one perfect diet that would melt off her pounds, get her in shape for her photo shoot, secure her the money she needed and get Charles and baby Charlie back.

She set aside the first bunch of diet books and went back to the bookstore.

She was lugging another half-dozen diet books through the mall when her cell phone rang.

"Hello," she said, breathless from the weight of the book bags and her own extra pounds.

"Cate, it's Gena," she said in the rushed manner Cate remembered so well. "I'm calling to let you know there's been a change in the date of the photo shoot for your book cover."

Cate felt the hand holding the phone go slick with sweat. Panic gripped her. She was beginning to have serious doubts that she would make her weight-loss goal in the time she had. There was no way she could do it in any less time. If she failed, she would lose her one chance to get Charles and her baby back.

"Cate, are you there?" Gena's impatient voice crackled over the sounds of traffic, impatient for Cate's reply.

"I'm still here," said Cate, braced for the worst.

"Where was I? This place is like Grand Central Station. Oh, yes, as I was saying, we're pushing back the publication date of the book into the new year and postponing the shoot for a couple of months. Catch you later."

Cate went limp with relief. Before she could say goodbye, Gena was gone. But she had left behind a gift of sixty precious days.

With renewed hope, Cate loaded the books into the car and drove home, eager to begin dieting and losing once again, this time she promised herself, with more success.

But Cate was new to dieting.

The Diet

She had no idea that she was now one of thousands of women who loaded diet books into their cars, drove home filled with resolve, good intentions and hope, only to fail.

Cate was about to find out.

Chapter 43

Cate was losing her battle with fat.

In fact, she was losing all her battles.

By early fall, pressure was mounting from all sides. With only a month to the photo shoot, she wasn't even close to losing the ninety pounds she had set as her goal.

Her battle with Charles wasn't going well either. Hiding behind Mrs. Bea and her lawyer, Charles buried her under a mountain of legal documents.

Every request she made through her newly-hired lawyer to see baby Charlie brought a fresh storm of paperwork. Every phone call she made was intercepted by an answering machine. Even the gifts she sent were returned, unopened. Mrs. Bea had her family and Charles, slipping easily back into the safety of her home, resisted all of Cate's efforts.

That wasn't all. She learned that Charles, to punish her, hadn't paid the rent on *The Cookery* for months. He had also closed all their accounts and withdrew the last of their money.

The Diet

Finally, her lawyer was able to reinstate the accounts and force Charles to share their remaining savings with Cate.

But the legal maneuverings came too late to save *The Cookery*. The landlord revoked her lease and took back the building.

Cate lost her husband, her child and her business.

The only thing she wasn't losing was her fat.

Her depression came crashing back.

The Diet

Chapter 44

That's how Sam found her, in bed at two o'clock in the afternoon, the blinds pulled down and the floor littered with candy wrappers and discarded diet books.

"What happened?" Sam asked. "I thought you were going to pick me up at the airport. Is it the baby? Is she sick? Has Charles done something else?"

Cate was ashamed that her baby sister should see her in this state.

"Come on, Cate, sit up," bullied Sam. "Talk to me. What's wrong?"

"Everything's wrong," came the muffled answer from deep inside a pillow. "My life is totally falling apart."

"It can't be that bad," said Sam.

"Oh, yes it can," answered Cate, sitting up but pulling the covers up to her neck to hide her body. "Charles won't let me see Charlie. He won't even talk to me. I lost *The Cookery,* and I've only got thirty days left and forty-three pounds to lose before the photo shoot. It's hopeless."

The Diet

Then Cate told Sam about her plan to cash the check for the second half of her advance, get Charles and Charlie back and re-build her life.

"I can't help you with the money," Sam shrugged. "I gave it all to my diet guy and he's got it invested in his company. And as far as Charles goes, I don't know why you want him back, except that you always had this thing about family—you know, a mommy and a daddy, and kids.

"But I can help you with the weight," she continued as she stepped over the piles of diet books scattered on the floor around the bed and pulled the covers off Cate's head. "How much have you lost already?"

"Almost forty-seven pounds."

"That's great."

"No it's not. It took me about ten different diets and weeks to lose that much. How am I going to lose almost two pounds a day for the next month? That's all the time I've got left."

"Easy," said Sam, reaching into her shoulder bag and tossing a bottle of capsules on the bed, "just take a couple of these."

"What are these?" asked Cate, sitting up straighter.

"My new best friends," Sam said as she went into the bathroom, where she stripped out of her travel clothes and into a baby blue sports bra trimmed in white, a matching pair of sweat pants and a cropped jacket.

"They're the little miracles I just finished doing the television infomercial for. They're great. It's like they have

The Diet

fat radar. They go right to the fat and 'poof' it's gone. I lost eleven pounds practically overnight when I first started taking them. So come on. Get up. Put your running shoes on. You're going to get thin so fast, you won't believe it. And you won't have to do all those diets, either."

Sam came out of the bathroom holding a glass of water.

Cate took a good look at her. She had to admit that she looked wonderful. She was leaner than ever. Her eyes were bright. She was overflowing with energy. Maybe Sam was right. Maybe this was the solution.

"What's in them?" asked Cate, critically examining the two large colorful capsules she had shaken out of the bottle. "Are you sure they're safe?"

Sam took the bottle from Cate, shook four capsules into the palm of her hand and swallowed them down in one gulp.

"Sure. They're prescription. You can only get them from a doctor. My doctor makes them. See, I'm taking doubles and I'm not worried."

She thrust the glass of water at Cate.

Cate, hoping for a miracle, swallowed hers.

Five minutes later the two sisters were outside.

"Hey, wait for me," called Cate as Sam sprinted across the street and ahead into the park.

Feeling energized, Cate followed.

Gone were her usual sluggishness and the aches in her legs that accompanied most of her recent exercising

The Diet

efforts. Her head felt clear and her mood exuberant. Everything was sharper, more in focus. Even the air seemed crystal clear, intoxicating.

As she ran, hope returned.

The Diet

Chapter 45

She saw herself slender again. She saw her book piled in high stacks in bookstore windows across the country. She saw herself interviewed on national television.

With every step her wildest dreams became more real and she raced toward them.

She forgot she had lost *The Cookery* and saw it in the pink bubbles her brain was blowing, bursting with classes and food and wonderful gadgets.

She saw it doubling, then tripling, springing up all across the country in little *Cookery* franchises.

As she ran, she saw Charles smiling, his arm around her waist as together they stood over a crib, watching their sleeping daughter.

Lost in her own little capsule of daydreams, Cate rounded a bend and ran right into a crowd blocking her path.

She heard the shrill scream of an ambulance at exactly the same moment as she caught a glimpse of a baby blue leg and a tumble of golden hair.

The Diet

"Oh my God. Sam," she screamed, pushing the onlookers aside.

Sam lay sprawled across the path. Her legs were twisted and her arms outstretched. There were flecks of reddish foam in the corners of her mouth.

Cate, her heart pounding, scooped Sam up into her lap and pulled her close, rocking her the way she used to when her sister was little. Sam opened her eyes and managed a small smile. Then her eyes rolled back and her body went completely limp.

Even as she held her, Cate could feel Sam's life draining into the earth where she lay.

Chapter 46

There was an autopsy and an inquest.

Cate ate through both.

She learned for the first time that Sam had been taking diet pills for years.

She had started with one prescription that had severely damaged her heart valves. Her last experiment was with the diet cocktail in the colorful capsules, a newly approved prescription formula that had spiked her blood pressure and caused a massive and fatal coronary.

Cate ate before the funeral and then sat alone.

She was wracked with guilt.

"I killed Sam," she accused herself silently.

She looked at Sam's picture, in its simple silver frame on the coffin, and saw her sister as she was on the night they took their mother away to the morgue, a vulnerable five-year old looking up at her and solemnly repeating, "I will never be fat."

"It was my vow that killed Sam," wept Cate.

The Diet

Through her sorrow and her tears, she asked herself, "Where would it end? My mother is dead. My baby son is dead. Sam is dead."

In a moment of perfect clarity she saw their deaths linked by one thing and one thing alone.

Fat.

Chapter 47

Someone must have brought her home from the funeral, because when she woke up several hours later it was dark. She was on the couch covered with an afghan. On the floor beside her was a cold cup of tea.

She had a vague memory of a strong arm supporting her and a warm hand stroking back her hair.

Then reality crashed over her.

She was alone once more. In her loneliness her hunger returned. She craved the food that would dull her pain, fill her emptiness and calm her fear. She craved carbs.

With one hand already on the fridge, Cate stopped. No. She wouldn't give in to her body's terrible hunger for carbs. She had already lost too many she loved to the same enemy.

No, she vowed. She would begin to fight again.

This time she would win.

She would find the perfect diet.

The Diet

Chapter 48

Cate felt some of her old determination returning. She felt some of her old control coming back to her.

She had a plan.

First, she would get the photo shoot postponed. After all, *Middleton & March* had themselves postponed the shoot once; surely they would grant her the same privilege.

Then she would ignore all the diet books and simply stop eating. She would fast. Starvation would be her new diet.

Cate crossed her fingers and dialed Gena's number but her courage failed her. She hung up on the first ring.

A few minutes later she tried again. This time she made her request—to Gena's voice mail.

"Gena, it's Cate. I have a small favor to ask. I need a little more time to…well…to be…to be myself again," she stammered but plowed bravely on. "Would it be possible to postpone the cover photo shoot for another month or even three weeks? That would really help me. Thank you." Cate broke the connection.

The Diet

Next she stepped on the scale. There were sixty-six pounds to lose. She had gained back twenty-three pounds.

Then she had made an elaborate chart with different colored markers labeling pounds, inches and deadline dates.

Two hours later she postponed her idea of starvation and popped a couple of slices of bread into the toaster. Waiting for her toast, she arranged and re-arranged her diet books. She was going to piece together some plan that would work.

Like all dieters, she would begin tomorrow.

She was still working and snacking four hours later when the doorbell rang. It was Gena.

The Diet

Chapter 49

"Cate, I'm not going to beat around the bush. *Middleton & March* is canceling your book contract."

"Gena, please..."

"Why didn't you tell me about this weight thing of yours sooner? I could have done something."

"Gena, listen to me please. I've already lost almost thirty pounds. I know I can lose the rest. All I need is a little more time."

"There is no more time. Anyway, it's out of my hands. Jim Cleary, the CFO of *Middleton & March*, recently bought a big house in River Hills. He and his wife were shopping at that gourmet market you always bought your stuff in. They saw you. He called Fred Leech, the publisher, and Fred called me ten minutes after I got your message." Her tone was bitter.

"Gena, I'm so sorry. Isn't there something you can do?" asked Cate, the desperation in her voice growing. "Can't you postpone the project until the spring, or even next year?"

The tears Cate fought to control threatened to spill over her lashes and down her cheeks.

"I'm sorry too," Gena said, her tone softening. "Fred was furious that I hadn't kept a closer eye on you. When they dropped you *Middleton & March* cancelled me as well. I was supposed to be on top of this project and I wasn't."

Gena put her hand over Cate's. "It's over, Cate, for both of us."

Then she turned her own brimming eyes away from Cate's anguished ones and delivered the final blow.

"I've been instructed to tell you the company is going to demand the return of all the advance money already paid to you."

With that she turned, walked to her car, got in, and drove away.

Cate stood in the doorway and began to shake from fear.

With the book gone, so was her hope for getting Charles and Charlie back.

She was broke and worse, she was in debt. She had spent the past months living off her credit cards until their joint account had been re-opened. The legal bills had mounted. She believed she would be fine for money and could pay everything off once she got the rest of her advance.

Her life in pieces, everyone and everything she ever loved lost to her, she decided to end it all.

She decided to eat herself to death.

The Diet

Chapter 50

"Good decision," she thought. "Death by carbs is definitely the way to go."

Cate believed this was her heritage, her reality and her fate.

She had finished the cookies, the ice cream and the cold spaghetti and still those carb cravings kept right on pushing her to eat more. For the first time in months she was grateful to them. They would make her goal that much easier to achieve.

"Five more minutes to the pizza delivery," Cate thought impatiently as she picked bits of spaghetti off the counter.

Panic was beginning to set in.

In carb deprivation, she leaned her head against the cold door of the fridge and sent up one final desperate prayer: "Help me. I can no longer help myself."

Just then doorbell rang. She scooped up some money and opened the door.

Josh stood in the harsh overhead light of the porch. His arms were loaded with pizza boxes and cinnamon bun containers. Balanced on top was a stack of file folders.

"Listen," he said, "I need a food writer, and I hear you need a job. Read the stuff in these folders and see what you can do with it."

He shoved the entire mess into her arms and raising his hand, gently brushed a strand of damp hair off her forehead.

"By the way, the pizza's on me." Then he was gone.

The Diet

Chapter 51

Cate watched him walk out of the circle of light and into the darkness.

Even though her face burned with humiliation that he had seen her like this, a fat failure, there came to her a wisp of memory of a hand holding up a cup of tea, pulling up an afghan and stroking her head after Sam's funeral.

Waves of shame rolled over her again. She had treated him badly.

"How disappointed he must be in me," she thought, "but not half as disappointed as I am in myself."

And with that thought, she turned and stepped back into the house.

The Diet

The Diet

Part Two

The Diet

The Diet

Chapter 52

Hot tears of shame and self-disgust dropped in big salty stains on Cate's oversized top.

She stumbled back to the safety of the kitchen, thinking of the only comfort left to her, the contents of the boxes in her arms. But in her rush, she caught her foot on a chair. Pizza, cinnamon buns and file folders went flying.

Defeated, she slid down the wall and sat on the floor, right in the middle of the mess. She reached across the floor, picked up a torn slice of pizza, blew on it, and took a big bite.

The carbs flooded through her like a painkiller.

She couldn't get enough. She ate a second piece, this one sweetened around the edges with spilled frosting.

By her third slice, she had calmed down enough to make a half-hearted effort at scooping up the spilled folders and papers.

She glanced briefly at each sheet as she set it down in a not very tidy pile on the floor beside her.

Many had notes in the margins, written in the almost indecipherable shorthand Josh used.

"He must have been collecting this stuff for months," she thought, surprised that he apparently never replaced her with a new food writer.

One article had a small envelope clipped to it. Cate opened it. Josh had written her a check and a note that read, "For your first article."

She was wracked with a fresh wave of guilt and shame. He was so good to her. He still believed in her. And here she sat unable to do anything but eat and mindlessly pick up other people's articles off her floor.

Unable to resist, she glanced at some of the headlines. *The Low-Carb Shopping List—Surprise Additions* one title teased. Hooked, she skimmed it. There were no surprises.

Another promised *Ten Ways To Turn Fat Fast Food into Low-Carb Fast Food,* but started with the tired suggestion to "lose the buns."

"Give me a break," she thought bitterly. "This stuff must have been written by people who never had a single carb craving in their entire lives."

Developing Carb Resistance testified a bold headline in a scholarly journal.

"There is no resistance to carbs," Cate muttered, with the resignation of the addicted.

"No matter how much will power, resolve or motivation I have, carbs always win. It doesn't matter whether they are low carbs or not. It isn't possible to stop

The Diet

after just one bite. The first cookie means the whole package. One potato chip means the whole bag. And every single carb means calories. Every single calorie means fat. That's the reality of carbs."

Best Carbs For Dieters. This was torn from a popular magazine with a scribble in the margin from Josh, "idea for article...give to Cate."

"What does Josh know? There are no 'best carbs for dieters'," Cate decided, and tossed the article on the pile with all the rest.

No matter what diet she tried carbs did her in every time. Her carb cravings were demons shaking her with uncontrollable longing, never leaving her alone, exploiting her every vulnerability, stalking her by day, waking her up at night.

"Just like my mother," she reminded herself as she reached for her fourth slice of pizza.

But then the words *Carb Secrets* in flowing slender script caught her attention. Despite herself she began to read, hoping a carb secret would be revealed to her, a revelation that would give her power over carbs the way they had power over her. But there were no secrets.

The article landed on the top of the pile with all the others, and Cate reached for another slice of pizza. There was less than half a pizza left and just one bulging folder still spilled on the floor.

"Carb secrets," she sighed. "If only...."

Chapter 53

A headline—*The Positive Effects of Zero-Calorie Carbohydrates on Craving Suppression, Fullness and Weight Loss*—from an obscure journal caught her eye.

The zero-calorie carb bit got her attention first.

"A zero-calorie carb?" she wondered. "That's different. That's better than low carb, surely?"

She let her pizza-soaked imagination drift.

"Was there really such a thing? Was there really a carb that had no calories?"

She looked at the title more carefully.

She shook herself alert.

She almost couldn't believe what she was reading.

It seemed that headline was written just for her.

Intrigued, she put down her half-eaten slice of pizza, pulled the journal out of its folder and began to read very slowly and very carefully.

What Cate read that dark night was the long-sought answer to her prayers.

Chapter 54

The pizza lay congealed on the floor. The cinnamon buns, forgotten, had gone dry. The spilled frosting had hardened.

Cate stretched her aching back and leaned back against the wall. She had been reading for two hours.

The article about zero-calorie carbs gripped her imagination. She read it three times. Then she read the rest of the articles in the journal.

Cate closed her eyes and thought about everything she had just read.

She tried to become the journalist she had once been.

She tried to be dispassionate, but she was gripped by the kind of excitement that only a new idea can bring.

She was hooked on this wonder carb.

She went back to that first article once again.

It described the joint efforts of two teams of university researchers—one in the United States and one in Europe—who had been researching a carb unlike any other. This carb had no calories.

The Diet

"This carbohydrate, or carb, once ingested, passes through the body's digestive system," explained the lead American scientist, "and because it has no calories of its own, it leaves no calories behind in the body to become fat. In fact, we believe it may also act as a kind of internal scrub brush, removing calories left by other carbohydrates."

Another researcher called it, "a kind of "non-stick carb."

A third, a female biochemist with a flair for simplifying complex concepts, described it as "a perfect carb, free of calories, free of fat and free of fear."

Cate got it.

With her own flair for words, she turned the clumsy and long, zero-calorie carb into the quick, fast and immediately memorable cal-free carb.

"This could become my favorite carb," she said aloud.

Cate's reading didn't end there.

There were still more exciting articles in the folder.

One described the ability of the cal-free carb to create the comfort of fullness that lasted for hours.

Another talked about how the cal-free carb sent signals to the brain and remotely shut off all cravings like the new satellite systems that could turn off the engine in a speeding stolen car.

With each article, Cate's excitement grew.

When she read about the cookie experiment her instincts about food, so long dulled, sharpened once again.

The Diet

A group of carb researchers made a big, fat, sweet, chocolate-chip cookie.

They found that the cookie was loaded with a whopping twenty-five grams of fat-making traditional carbs.

That's when they did the big carb switch.

They replaced the fat-making traditional carbs in the original cookie dough with the new cal-free carbs.

Now they had a whole new cookie. It was still the same size and gave that same wonderful cookie satisfaction. But it didn't make any new fat. Loaded with cal-free carbs, here was a cookie that could help a person lose fat.

This was the miracle that offered all the comfort and satisfaction of carbs with none of the guilt and none of the fat.

For the first time in months, Cate dared to hope.

Could this little cal-free carb give Cate back everything all those other carbs had taken from her? Could this tiny miracle bring back her shape, her family and her future?

Cate was determined to find out.

Chapter 55

"I can use this cal-free carb to free myself of cravings. I can use it to eat myself back into the body I had," Cate realized. "With this cal-free carb I can even cook myself back into the life I used to have."

As she struggled to her feet she reminded herself, "This is about writing and reporting. That's what I do. But this is also about food. That's also what I know."

Realizing that the combination of the two, writing and cooking, could change her life once more, she told herself, "I can cook with this cal-free carb. I can write about it. I can make it work for me. I can lose all my fat with it. I can use it to save my life."

Cate no longer felt like a victim trapped in a prison of fat she had eaten herself into. With renewed strength and confidence, Cate felt like herself once more.

Chapter 56

Cate knew she was on to something.

Energized and motivated, she threw out the pizza and scraped up the sugary mess of the buns.

She found her imported coffee maker and took out the exotic blend of African and South American coffee she kept in her freezer.

While the coffee brewed, Cate rummaged through the kitchen drawers until she found a clean, empty notebook.

She placed the notebook squarely on the table. Next she lined up all the articles she had read and sharpened a handful of pencils.

She poured coffee into a fragile china cup with a delicate matching saucer. The days of big bulky mugs for Cate were over. She was ready to begin.

She sat down, opened the notebook and wrote *My Diet Diary* on the first page.

"Let's do it," she said to the diary, "let's create the perfect diet."

Chapter 57

Cate sipped her coffee and chewed on the end of her pencil. Then she began to write, self-consciously and halting at first, then gathering speed and confidence.

"Dear Diet Diary." she wrote, and then rubbed it out.

"Diet Diary is too formal," she decided. "I'm going to call you D.D. Okay, D.D. Let's get started."

"What do I want my perfect diet to do?" she wrote on the first line.

"I want my perfect diet to solve my biggest problem, which is losing weight," she answered on the second line.

And then she stopped and put down the pencil.

"That's not true," she admitted to herself. "Losing weight is not my biggest problem at all. I've lost weight lots of times, on lots of different diets. My biggest problem is keeping the weight off. I need to turn off the fat switch and stop the cravings. My biggest problem is stopping my body from making new fat faster than I can lose the old fat."

The Diet

Cate took another sip of the stimulating coffee, picked up her pencil again and this time wrote,
> My perfect diet has to do two things:
> 1. It has to get rid of all my fat.
> 2. It has to stop making new fat.

Chapter 58

"First, D.D.," wrote Cate, "let's you and me look at losing fat."

She collected all the diet books she had bought and organized them in neat piles on the kitchen table.

There was the one that came with suggestions for pre-packaged foods. She spent $200 on the food and lost only four pounds. That was about $50 a pound.

Next were the books that promoted a diet low in fat. She lost only twelve pounds and then stalled.

Recognizing that carbs were her biggest problem, she tried the most popular of the carb diets and gained back six of the pounds she had lost previously. She found that with her first bite of any carb all control flew out the window.

She tried diets linked to genetics, biology, women's studies and even business plans. She lost another slow fourteen pounds and promptly gained back seven.

She tried diets proposed by doctors, psychologists, and national agencies and organizations with equally disappointing results.

The Diet

Finally, in desperation, she tried the high-protein diets. Steak, chicken, and cheese for fourteen days led to a quick and dramatic weight loss of twenty-one pounds. Then she suffered carb withdrawal so severe it woke her up in the middle of the night and drove her to the fridge. There she stood, stuffing whatever carbs she could find into her mouth as fast as possible.

Cate succeeded in losing weight with each diet, but none of them could stay far enough ahead of the new fat her body was making.

Chapter 59

"Okay, D.D.," she wrote, "I need a two-part diet. The first part of the diet will help me lose all the fat I've already got. The second part will help me stop making new fat. That is where the cal-free carb can begin to work its magic.

"So, first I'll figure out the best weight-loss diet to team up with my new cal-free carb."

The fastest-working diet for her was the high-protein program. She lost fat pounds and fat inches and she lost them fast.

Obviously protein calories were major fat fighters.

Cate wrote in her diary:

"Part one is the high-protein part because protein calories burn off the fat I've already got stored. Part two is the cal-free carb part. Cal--free carbs have no calories, they don't make new fat, and they don't trigger those terrible cravings. I'll get carb satisfaction without carb fat."

Cate sat back, and re-read what she had written. It made sense.

The Diet

Now she had to turn it into a real diet, with real food she could eat, enjoy and lose weight on.

She felt in control. Powerful. She felt up to the challenge.

She added, "Dear D.D. I can do this."

The Diet

Chapter 60

It was that charcoal-gray hour between night and morning but Cate wasn't a bit tired. What was even more remarkable, she wasn't a bit hungry.

What she was, was hot, burning with ideas, feverishly writing, trying to get everything locked into the pages of her improvised diet diary.

"Okay, D.D.," she jotted on a clean page. "What's next? I think the next thing to do is develop lists of ingredients, foods I can use to create high-protein fat-burning recipes and menus.

"Once I've got those down, I can do the same thing and come up with lists of ingredients and foods high in cal-free carbs to create fat-blocking recipes and menus."

She started her protein list.

First, she wrote down all the high-protein meats she remembered: chicken, beef and turkey. She added others not as often seen on high-protein menus: veal, pork, lamb, duck, ham and Cornish hens.

Next, she made her dairy list. Here was the cream so much loved by high-protein advocates, along with

The Diet

cheeses such as, Cheddar, Swiss, Provolone and American. She added some of her own favorites: fresh juicy Mozzarella, creamy Brie and Camembert, sharp tangy goat cheese and biting Parmesan and Romano.

Then she added yogurt, milk and eggs.

The fish list was practically endless. Crispy-skinned Chilean sea bass, pink salmon and deep-rose tuna followed delicate Dover and lemon sole and hearty monkfish. There was flounder and haddock. There were shrimp, scallops, oysters, clams and lobster. The seas and rivers provided a watery harvest rich in fat-burning protein.

She drew a blank and had to refer back to the high-protein diet books to add nuts and bacon, sausages and tofu and the wonderful oil of the olive.

Her cal-free carb list was next.

She went back to the articles that had inspired her and found a list of the foods high in cal-free carbs. She copied it carefully into her diet diary.

First, there were fruits: apples, peaches, pears, oranges, grapefruits, lemons, limes, kiwi and every imaginable berry.

Second, there were vegetables: broccoli, beets, cabbage, celery, cauliflower, lettuce, peas, peppers, onions, snow peas, spinach, tomatoes, zucchini, cucumbers, radishes, even potatoes and more.

There were raisins, currants, figs and dates.

There were the grains, seeds and flours of the Bible and of science—wheat, oat, barley, rice, sunflower, soy and corn meal.

The Diet

She had her lists.
But then she got stuck and the doubt started.

The Diet

Chapter 61

Suddenly, in that most terrifying hour of the empty night, with only the hum of the fridge and her own beating heart to keep her company, what she was attempting to do seemed impossible.

Sitting at her kitchen table, surrounded by best-selling diet books, Cate felt fat and foolish and a failure.

"What am I thinking?" she asked herself. "I'm not a doctor, or a dietician, or even a nutritionist. Who am I to think I can come up with a perfect diet for myself when all these experts tried and failed?"

"Who am I to think that marrying these cal-free carbs to protein is going to work, that together they can block and burn fat? And if it is such a great idea, why hasn't someone else already written about it?"

Flipping through the pages, first of one diet book, then another with tired and cramped fingers, she began to regret throwing out the pizza and buns. She began to wonder if she should retrieve them from the garbage just as she had retrieved the spaghetti a few short hours ago. But she was too tired to move and too tired to think.

The Diet

But she wasn't too tired to cry.

She cried for the Cate she used to be, the slim happy, successful Cate who gloried in food, who loved to create new recipes and menus, the Cate who adored teaching and learning about food.

She wept because that Cate was gone, buried under a mountain of fat. Buried under that same mountain were her family and the life she lost.

She wept because all that was left was this sad, fat woman who a few minutes ago actually thought she could create a diet.

The pages of her diary grew soggy and smudged as her tears fell on them, and still she wept.

"Who am I kidding?" she sobbed, "so what if I found that protein calories burned off my fat? So what if I believe that cal-free carbs will help my body to stop making new fat? So what if I believe that protein and cal-free carbs together could be the perfect diet? Who am I, this fat failure, to think I have any kind of an answer?"

Finally, she was wept dry.

But still she couldn't get the protein and cal-free carbs combo out of her head. A sliver of possibility that she had actually found something that would really work refused to wash away with her tears.

She rode her stomach-churning emotional roller coaster. Up with elation. Down with despair. Filled briefly with excitement and the hope of success, she was then overwhelmed by the fear of failure.

The Diet

Emotionally exhausted, she sighed, "What I need is a sign, something to show me I'm on the right track."

The Diet

Chapter 62

In a frenzy of lost hope, she stood in front of her kitchen bookshelf and started to pull down all the cookbooks she had collected over the years, letting them spill open on the floor at her feet.

That's when the card fell out.

She recognized it immediately.

The man with the kind eyes picked it up that terrible night from beside her mother's body and handed it to her. When the lady from foster care packed their things, she had tucked it into an old cookbook belonging to Cate's mother. Cate kept the cookbook all those years. Unused and forgotten, the book was one of the very few possessions her mother left.

The little card, no bigger than the palm of her hand, brought back a flood of memories.

Her mother didn't go to church regularly but she did tell Bible stories to Cate and Sam, reciting them from memory while they traced the story with small children's fingers on little cards. This story and this picture card had been one of Cate's favorites.

The Diet

On one side of the small printed card was a picture of a low hilltop. Palm trees waved against a light-blue sky. A scattered crowd sat on green grass. Men carried large flat baskets. A solitary figure, with long flowing hair and dressed in a white robe, stood on the crest of the hill.

Cate turned the card over. There were two illustrations in black and white of five loaves and two fishes.

All at once Cate felt a power deep inside herself, a voice resonating.

Not trusting her own memory, she took the card upstairs to the Bible she kept in her bedside table. She flipped rapidly through the pages until she found the passage she was looking for.

And she read those beautiful words to the story of the loaves and fishes.

"As evening approached, the disciples came to him and said, "This is a remote place, and it's already getting late. Send the crowds away, so they can go to the villages and buy themselves some food."

Jesus replied, "They do not need to go away. You give them something to eat."

"We have here only five loaves of bread and two fish," they answered.

"Bring them here to me," he said. And he directed the people to sit down on the grass. Taking the five loaves and the two fishes and looking up to heaven, he gave thanks and broke the loaves. Then he gave them to his disciples, and the disciples gave them to the people. They

The Diet

all ate and were satisfied, and the disciples picked up twelve basketfuls of broken pieces that were left over. The number of those who ate was about five thousand men, besides women and children."

The loaves and the fishes. The cal-free carb and the protein. Together they made the perfect diet.

Cate had been given her sign.

Chapter 63

Strength returned to Cate. She was validated.
Picking up her pencil she wrote in her diary.
"I can learn from all the experts. But I can read for myself. I can think for myself. And with the help of the good Lord, I'm going to trust myself."

As she wrote, she felt the power of confidence, lightness of hope and the warmth of love filling her heart. And she felt something else.

For the first time since she was twelve-years old, she felt her mother's hand reaching out to her. She was her mother's child once again. The coldness and anger she had stored deep inside herself for so long began to soften and melt. Cate let go and she didn't fall. Her mother caught her.

Chapter 64

Cate propped the little loaves and fishes card on the table in front of her.

"How do I begin?" she asked herself. "How do I eat my proteins and my cal-free carbs? Should I eat them separately? Should I mix them up together? Should I alternate them? If I alternated them, which should I eat first?"

Stumped, she turned for help to the food lists.

"There is everything I ever loved to eat on these lists. All I have to do is cook it, eat it and lose weight."

But first she had to find a way to organize it. How to put them together?

Once again she could feel the slow ebbing away of her confidence, like standing water seeping around a clogged drain. She knew if she lost those precious drops of confidence and determination she would be left with her old emptiness.

Cate was suddenly very afraid because that old emptiness could only be filled with fat carbs. She could already feel the old familiar pull of those cravings.

The Diet

"Come on, diary," she demanded. "Help me. How do I begin?"

Once again, frustration and despair crashed over Cate.

Chapter 65

It was dawn. Cate's night of discovery and hope was coming to an end. Gray light slipped through cracks in the curtains and around the edges of the blinds, staining the counters with a shadowy film.

Discouraged, defeated and tired, Cate felt the victory she had won slipping away from her and the old cravings returning.

She had come far, but not far enough.

"It's hopeless," she despaired. "I'll never be able to put these two fat fighters together in a way that will work."

Her old remedy for frustration and relief began to torment her. She approached the fridge to gratify her urge when an ear-splitting ringing startled her, followed by a loud crash.

Cate hurried upstairs to look for the source of the din. She found it in her bedroom. There, toppled over on the floor, was her battered alarm clock.

That's when the answer hit her.

She knew exactly how to make the fat burning proteins and the cal-free carbs work together.

The Diet

The answer was in the clock.

She kissed its old cracked face in gratitude.

She knew with a clarity and sureness how these two powerhouses would work together. Each would support the other to defeat fat pounds once and for all.

She would let the clock help her turn back time and tick her back into slenderness, health and her perfect life.

"Come on, old friend," she said to the old clock, "let's go and get thin!"

Chapter 66

Drenched in a shower of inspiration, Cate felt like Cinderella, Tinkerbell and Mary Poppins all in one.

Propping the clock beside her loaves and fishes picture, she pulled the diet diary toward her once again.

She now knew exactly how she would organize her diet for success.

"Dear D.D.," she wrote with renewed faith and strength.

"My diet is going to follow the most ancient of rhythms. I'm going to organize every food day according to the natural division of the day, the A.M. hours followed by the P.M. hours. I'm going to start eating when the sun comes up. I'm going to stop eating when the sun goes down. I'm going to lose my fat second-by-second, minute-by-minute and hour-by-hour all day long.

"Because my first priority is to stop making new fat, my eating day will begin with foods rich in cal-free carbs, foods that will help me shut off my fat switch. I will eat to block fat in the A.M. hours.

"Then I will switch to protein to start burning off all my old stored fat. I will eat to burn fat in the P.M. hours."

With an instinct as deep and as true as the cycles of the sun and the moon and the stars, Cate knew she was right.

The Diet

Chapter 67

Her diet day easily fell into place. She would set her alarm clock six times a day.

As soon as she opened her eyes in the morning and felt the first temptation of cravings, she would take a big bite of a cal-free carb.

Then, with the terrible temptation soothed, she would calmly begin her cal-free carb breakfast.

If she got hungry during the morning, she would snack on more cal-free carbs until the hunger passed.

When the hands of her faithful old clock moved past noon, she would put aside her cal-free carbs. She would trust that her own body had turned off the fat-making switch and had stopped making new fat

She would then begin to burn off the fat she had made and stored. She would eat herself thin with a lunch of protein, followed by an afternoon protein snack, and finally, a generous protein-rich dinner.

Her body would begin to shed fat and once again she would be thin and healthy.

The Diet

Chapter 68

"I can do this," Cate knew. "I can really do this."

She was on familiar territory. This was about food and recipes and menus. This was what Cate was good at.

"O.K. D.D., let's get all my food organized. Let's start with getting A.M. thin." In big bold letters she wrote A.M. across the top of the page.

With that, Cate turned back to the food lists she had made, scrutinized them carefully, checked off foods that she could start her day with, and began to write.

"I'll call the first meal I eat every morning my Rise & Shine meal," she wrote. "I'll start my fat-stopping day with an orange or a pear or an apple or a bowl of berries, all filled to overflowing with cal-free carbs.

"No more skipping meals," Cate promised herself. "I'm going to have a proper breakfast. I'll have whole-grain breads, or pancakes, or waffles or cereals and more fruit, all loaded with cal-free carbs."

Breakfast would be her second meal of the day.

"If get hungry before lunch," she told herself, "I won't panic or reach for a candy bar, I'll snack on popcorn, whole-wheat crackers, fruit, pretzels, breads or more cereal."

The Morning Snack would be her third meal of the day.

Chapter 69

Next, Cate turned to what she would eat to get P.M. thin when the hands of her clock reached up and past noon.

"Lunch could be a thick meaty soup," she decided. "Or I can have unimaginable varieties of salads. There are egg dishes from scrambled eggs to elaborate omelets and soufflés. Meats and fish of every variety are possible. Lunch is a fat-burning bounty."

Lunch would be her fourth meal of the day.

"If I get hungry in the afternoon," she pledged in the pages of her diary. "I'm not going to deny myself food. I can snack on nuts, or flavored yogurt or a wedge of cheese."

The Afternoon Snack would be her fifth meal of the day.

"Now, D.D., let's do dinner."

She noted her selections of meats and poultry and fish, the dishes and combinations limited only by her talent and imagination.

Dinner would be her sixth meal of the day.

Chapter 70

Fingers cramped and aching, Cate sat back and looked at what she had written and made an exciting observation.

All the foods she had written down for her A.M. meals were naturals for the morning hours.

All the foods she had written down for her P.M. hours were naturals for the afternoon and the dinner hour.

Here was yet another validation that her diet was the right diet.

Suddenly the page she was writing on was flooded with light. Cate looked up. The sun had chased away the last of the dark night and the chilly gray dawn and was pouring its light through her kitchen window.

It was morning. She would begin right now.

"Dear diary," she wrote. "My diet—Day One."

The Diet

Chapter 71

The alarm clock rang announcing her Rise & Shine meal.

Humming a little to herself, Cate opened the fridge and automatically reached for the orange juice.

She stopped, the carton in her hand.

One of the most surprising things she had read was that orange juice had all the cal-free carbs squeezed out of it, as did apple juice, and every other kind of juice.

"Never drink juice if you want the benefit of these calorie-free carbs," warned the article. "Always eat the whole fruit." Cal-free carbs hid deep in the rich meat of fruit, in the pulpy fiber.

Remembering what she had read, Cate poured the juice down the drain.

She looked inside the fridge for a whole fruit.

One small solitary orange sat in the fruit bin along with a couple of apples and a slightly shriveled kiwi fruit. Cate grabbed the orange and shut the fridge door.

With a sharp paring knife she cut a small circle from the stem side. Then, slipping the sharp knife easily between the skin and the flesh, she stripped away the peel and exposed the bright orange center.

Again, wielding her paring knife like the expert she was, Cate quickly separated the sections, freeing them from the hard membrane, ridges and seeds.

She took down her fanciest dessert plate and arranged the glistening sections in a double fan.

She broke off a small mint leaf growing in a pot on her kitchen sill and placed it in the center of the orange fan. She admired the beautiful effect for a moment, then lifted an orange section and took a bite.

The sweetness of the icy cold orange burst in her mouth and trickled down her throat. Chewing the firm flesh, she thought of sunshine, frosty summer popsicles and enormous shiny golf umbrellas.

That orange was a happy food. It made her feel good inside and out.

It was the first food she had eaten that tasted pure and clean. It was the first food she wasn't afraid to enjoy.

It was good to eat without fear or guilt again.

It took her a long time to finish every single section of orange, much longer than it would have taken to guzzle down a big glass of orange juice.

With every orangey bite, Cate felt her whole body responding to the cal-free carbs. She could almost feel the fat-making process slowing down.

Chapter 72

With the fresh cool taste of the orange still on her tongue, she turned her attention to the A.M. list of cal-free carb ingredients to see what she could make for her first breakfast.

But then she realized that she didn't feel those cravings that usually overtook her the minute she put one piece of food into her mouth. She felt full and satisfied. She wasn't out-of-control hungry. Breakfast could wait.

As she put her plate into the dishwasher she glanced down and imagined herself slim and slender, the rolls of fat a distant memory.

Noticing her stained shirt, Cate suddenly felt embarrassed. The fatter she got, the less care she had taken about her clothes and her appearance.

"Time to get cleaned up," Cate ordered herself. She picked up her diary and pencil and marched herself up to the bathroom.

There she had a hot shower, washed her hair, put on make-up and sprayed a little cloud of perfume around her head. Pink and clean and naked, she stepped on the scale.

The scale read one hundred and eighty-seven pounds but Cate actually smiled to herself in the mirror.

"No problem," she said confidently. "This is where I begin."

Chapter 73

She padded back into the bedroom.

On a fresh page of the diary, using an elegant fountain pen she hadn't used in over a year, she wrote the day, Thursday, and the date, October 5.

It was almost one year to the day she had first confirmed that she was pregnant. A year ago she got her first book contract and took her first bite down the long and painful road to obesity.

There was a satisfying kind of symmetry to the date.

A year ago the date signified a new beginning. A year later it signified a new beginning of a different kind.

She wrote down her weight, 187 pounds, and her size 1X.

Next, Cate took out a faded red fabric tape measure and wrapped it around her naked hips. She noted down 49 ½ inches, then jotted down her other measurements.

Her waist was 39 inches, her bust 48 inches. Her thighs were 29 inches and her upper arms were 18 inches.

Then she pulled on a clean pair of elastic-waisted pants and a fresh oversized shirt.

Looking at herself in the mirror, she made a silent promise. "Only a little while longer and I'll be tucking in my shirts again and cinching my waist with leather belts."

Twisting and turning in the mirror, Cate could imagine herself slender and fine.

The clock rang, signaling her next meal.

With a final twirl and a last smile at herself in the mirror, Cate went downstairs for the first breakfast of her new diet.

The Diet

Chapter 74

Cate turned to the food lists of cal-free carbs she had so carefully compiled. Running her finger down the lists, she looked for a cal-free carb food that would work for her breakfast.

She found oatmeal. Cate gave a little grimace. Oatmeal was not high on her list of favorite foods. She was just about to take down the round tin of quick-cooking oats and find a saucepan when she got an idea.

"What if I turn the oatmeal into fat-blocking cookies? If the scientists could do it, so can I."

She quickly assembled the ingredients and made up the recipe as she went along.

First, she took down a big ceramic bowl and poured in one cup of all-purpose flour, one-quarter cup of the quick-cooking oats, three-quarters of a teaspoon of baking soda and a generous dash of ground cinnamon. She stirred the mixture together until it turned a pale ivory flecked with brown.

Next, she pulled out her electric mixer and in a second bowl creamed together two tablespoons of butter and six packets of artificial sweetener.

Just as it reached the ideal stage of soft peaks, she broke an egg into the mixture and beat it again until the egg disappeared.

Inspired by her food lists and wanting to fill her morning cookies with as many cal-free carbs as she could, she took the two apples from the fridge and grated them into the mixture.

Satisfied that the consistency was just right, she added the dry ingredients to the moist.

Wanting even more of the cal-free carbs, she pried open the lid of a canister, reached inside and then tossed a handful of golden raisins into the dough.

"A fine cook I've become," she scolded herself. "I forgot to preheat the oven."

She turned the oven dial to three hundred and seventy-five degrees and soon the little red indicator light turned on. The oven was ready.

Minutes later the kitchen was filled with the wonderful smell of warm cinnamon and apples.

Cate put on a new pot of coffee and when the cookies were ready she couldn't wait for them to cool. Sliding two onto her plate and the rest onto a wire rack, Cate poured herself a cup of coffee and bit into her improvised oatmeal cookie. It was delicious.

Cate felt thinner already.

The Diet

Chapter 75

Refreshed by her breakfast, Cate decided to take her diet all the way. She would give her kitchen a special A.M./P.M. makeover.

"I'll start with carbs," she decided. "I'll keep only foods that fit into my new A.M. cal-free carb category and that stop my body from making new fat. All other fat-makers will get tossed.

"I'll do exactly the same with my P.M. foods. I'll organize all the proteins and get rid of any that don't help my body burn fat."

As she attacked the fridge, Cate wrote down each food toss faithfully in her diet diary.

All the jars of fatty salad dressings, and bottles of ketchup, half-finished juices and sugary sodas were emptied and tossed into a big green garbage bag.

Next she scrubbed out every shelf and drawer.

Then she put back the few foods that belonged in her clean and sweet-smelling fridge.

The Diet

Into her fruit bin went the kiwi, a couple of lemons and a small clove of garlic. A bottle of low-sodium soy sauce was replaced on the narrow door shelf.

She returned a small chunk of Cheddar, a piece of blue cheese and a block of Parmesan along with a pint of heavy cream and half a carton of eggs. A container of olives went back too.

The only vegetable she had was a small iceberg lettuce. She cleaned the lettuce, packed it into a large plastic bag, and placed it in the vegetable bin. She left a Vidalia onion and a small soft tomato in a basket on the kitchen counter.

Next she tackled the freezer.

She quickly sorted through the frozen foods and kept the bags of broccoli, spinach, and peas with pearl onions, but tossed out all the vegetables in thick buttery sauces, as well as the economy-size bag of frozen French fries.

She kept a package of fish fillets but threw out batter-dipped fish. She also kept the ground beef and the ground veal.

That done, she looked at her fridge. It was emptier than it had ever been.

Next she started on her pantry and cupboards.

This turned out to be a massive undertaking.

With an empty garbage bag at her side, she stripped the shelves of pre-sweetened cereals, pastas, boxes of white rice, jars of spaghetti sauces, cans of sweetened fruit, and her old standby, chips.

The Diet

All she was left with was vinegar, olive oil, spices and herbs, brown rice, a half-empty box of artificial sweetener, a box of green tea and two cans of tuna.

Her kitchen makeover halfway done, she lugged out the two green garbage bags filled with food she no longer wanted or needed.

Chapter 76

It was a little after ten o'clock in the morning.

She felt the small rumblings in her tummy that usually signified a major carb attack.

Again, the faithful alarm rang right on time for her next meal. Cate reached for another two oatmeal cookies, a handful of raisins and the kiwi. Here was her first delicious Morning Snack.

"This is great," she acknowledged. "It's not even lunchtime and I've had already had three wonderful meals."

She made a personal note in her diary under Day One. "I feel terrific. I don't have any cravings. I feel satisfied. That hollow, empty feeling that used to be there in the pit of my stomach until I filled it full of carbs is gone. I actually feel like I've stopped making new fat. I feel calmer, like the fat-making engine is quiet. I can hardly wait to see how I feel after my P.M. meals."

The Diet

Chapter 77

Fortified with confidence, she was ready to begin her shopping list.

Turning to a fresh sheet in her diet diary, she wrote at the top of the page, My Cal-Free Carb List and began.

First came all the fruit, fresh, frozen and canned.

She began with apples, followed by unsweetened applesauce.

Next came oranges, grapefruit and more kiwi.

Cate decided she would also treat herself to a pint each of strawberries, raspberries and blueberries. She would heap them in layers into a parfait glass and garnish the top with a slice of orange.

She added a few plums to stew in a little boiling water. Simmered with whole cloves, the fruit would turn into a thick compote.

Next came a can of pineapple in its own juices. She would broil a ring lightly dusted with cinnamon or nutmeg and fill the center with warm preserves.

Dates, to be stuffed with a tangy, slightly bitter Seville orange marmalade, went on her list.

The Diet

Since it was autumn, she would buy fresh pears or figs that she would cut into small slices, arrange across a layer of raspberry jam, top with a shake of ground ginger and bake.

Raisins and currants rounded out the fruit selections.

Next came whole-grain flour and corn meal, followed by cereals and grains. Then she added wheat germ and oat bran. These she would mix with all her other grains to boost their fat-stopping power.

Her head was spinning with all the breakfast breads and pastries and muffins she would bake, from a plain homespun, bran muffin to an exotic olive bread to enjoy for a morning snack with thick slices of tomato, to a pink cranberry bread bursting with succulent berries.

She added a loaf of raisin bread and a package of whole-grain English muffins to keep in the freezer and use one at a time. She would spread the English muffins with her *Cookery* jams and preserves.

She remembered seeing whole-wheat waffles in the grocery store and added a package of those to her list.

Then there was corn for popping, assorted grain crackers and pretzels. These she would pour into plastic bags and shake with garlic powder or chili pepper. Or she could add herbs like rosemary, shake the mixture up with Parmesan, and bake the mixture for a few minutes to create her own morning munchies.

As the crowning touch to her list, she added four spices—cloves, nutmeg, ginger and cinnamon—for her

The Diet

special Cate Spice Blend. One teaspoon of each mixed together would turn baked goods and cooked fruits into fragrant treats.

As she finished the last item, the alarm clock sounded again.

She had set the clock for just after noon. The cal-free carb morning was over. She had stopped making new fat.

Now it was time to switch over to proteins and start burning off all that old fat she had been storing for over a year.

Cate turned her attention to her first fat-burning lunch.

The Diet

Chapter 78

Rummaging around in the fridge, Cate realized that there wasn't much left after the makeover.

Challenged and inspired, she grabbed the iceberg lettuce. Then she took the overripe tomato and the Vidalia onion and chopped them together in a bowl. To this she added a few drops of olive oil, a pinch of sea salt, some freshly ground pepper and a quarter of a cup of blue cheese.

Taking a large white china dinner plate, she lined it with a few leaves of the lettuce. This would be the palette on which she would build her lunch. Already the contrast of the bright white plate and the soft green were beginning to tempt her.

"I'm going to make my own version of a Mediterranean salad," she realized as inspiration struck.

She added canned tuna to the center of the plate.

"I need a little contrasting color and more fat-burning protein," she said to herself and decided to hardboil an egg. After a quick rinse under cold water, she peeled it and chopped it very fine.

The Diet

She topped the tuna with the tomato, onion and cheese mixture. With a flourish, she garnished the top with a few sliced olives and the chopped hardboiled egg.

The colors—the pale green of the lettuce, the rich red of the tomato, the soft pink of the tuna and the gold, white and glistening black of the egg and olive—were pleasing and tempting.

She took out a linen napkin, poured a glass of ice water into one of her best wine goblets, and sat down to enjoy her lunch.

"When I'm thin again, Charles and I will sit in a café in France or Italy and have a salad like this one while the baby sleeps beside us," she daydreamed as she munched, savoring the textures and the flavors.

She didn't miss bread or other fat-making carbs. The meal was simple and delicious and she could feel her old fat melting away with every bite.

When she finished, she entered her lunch into her food diary, and then pulled her shopping list toward her.

The Diet

Chapter 79

Now it was time to write down all the P.M. foods that she needed to buy.

Blue cheese, Cheddar, Swiss, cottage cheese and Ricotta went on the list first.

These she would use in timbales, crust-free quiches made with whipped eggs, milk, cheese, and celery salt and baked until set. She would make larger ones for lunches and dinners and individual ones for snacks.

She also wrote down cream cheese, which she would mix with a spoonful or two of heavy cream and then fold in her favorite red currant preserves called Bar-le-Duc. This unique dish would make a satisfying afternoon snack.

Then came yogurt, plain and fruit-flavored and frozen. She added a half-pint of cream and a carton of skim milk.

She wrote down a small pork tenderloin, which she would divide into two dinners. She would roast half, rubbed with garlic and rosemary and bake it on a bed of sweet onions. The second half she would slice and stew in

The Diet

a skillet with crushed coriander seed, olives, mushrooms and a dash of lemon juice.

She added a small steak. She would grill it, enjoy one half, and save the second half to slice over a huge salad made with different kinds of lettuces.

She would buy a chicken, which would give her crispy-skinned dinners, fleshy white lunches, and would end up, bones and all, as the base for a clear sipping broth.

A boneless lamb roast was next. She would score the roast in a winged pattern and insert slivers of garlic and sprigs of fresh rosemary into each cut. Then she would rub the entire surface with olive oil, season it with freshly ground pepper and salt and roast it. The aroma of the lamb, garlic and rosemary would permeate the whole house and prove irresistible.

Two more cans of water-packed tuna, two cans of sardines and one of salmon for croquettes also made the list.

Next came a package of deli meats, assorted slices of ham, turkey and chicken.

A dozen eggs, a jar of crunchy peanut butter and a pound of assorted nuts—almonds, cashews, peanuts and pecans—were added and her P.M. shopping list was done.

Chapter 80

Now came all the free foods that she would need to create the A.M. and P.M. recipes for her diet.

Cate wrote down squash and cabbage. She added the delicate leaves of baby spinach, the crisp dark fronds of Romaine lettuce and the slightly bitter radicchio that she would season with olive oil, salt and pepper and grill to accompany her meat recipes.

She wrote down tomatoes, bunches of scallions and thick bulbs of yellow, white and purple onions, and one of her favorites, leeks.

She checked to make sure that she had plenty of spices and fresh herbs, especially flat-leaf parsley, dill, rosemary, basil and garlic.

She added balsamic vinegar and hot pepper and Worcestershire sauces to the list.

Then she was finished.

The Diet

Chapter 81

With her diet diary tucked firmly under her arm, Cate walked into the market.

It was late in the afternoon and she was once again beginning to feel those twinges that in the past had signaled a carb binge.

Today each twinge could be satisfied with her new approach to food.

She was in luck.

A small table was set out in the deli aisle. There was a platter with a selection of new cheeses. Lightly browned imported Italian sausages sat in a hot chafing dish. The aroma of garlic and oregano filled the section and Cate stopped at the display.

She accepted a small paper plate filled with cubed cheeses from different regions of Italy and thick chunks of the steaming sausages, from pale pink to deep burgundy, veined and beaded with opalescent rivulets and bubbles of fat.

Holding them delicately by the thin wooden picks and letting the flavor linger on her tongue, Cate really tasted and enjoyed each piece of cheese and each sausage.

The Diet

It was the best afternoon snack she could have imagined. It satisfied all her cravings for rich tastes and stilled the evil food voices before they could whisper "carbs."

The Diet

Chapter 82

With enormous satisfaction, Cate reviewed the first day of her new diet.

Her kitchen was restocked with both A.M. foods loaded with cal-free carbs that would help her body turn off the fat-making machinery, and high in protein P.M. foods that would begin to burn off her accumulated fat.

It had been a very long time since Cate had worked with such enthusiasm and passion in her kitchen. It had been a very long time since Cate had enjoyed the touch of food, the satisfaction and the joy of cooking and eating.

Just as she was about to sit down and write in her diary once again, the alarm clock rang signaling dinner.

She had planned to fix a small steak for her first diet day dinner, but the market had fresh salmon steaks. She bought one and poached it in a vegetable broth seasoned with a bouquet of parsley, dill and a bay leaf. She added half a dozen tiny scallops, broccoli spears, slivers of red and yellow sweet peppers, baby onions as tiny and perfect as crystal marbles and circles of finely sliced leeks.

The Diet

She served the dish in a large shallow bowl. The fish, the vegetables and the broth tasted of ocean waves and warm gardens.

Cate sighed with satisfaction. This had been a good day filled with fresh tastes and sensations of fullness, a day in which she controlled food.

Best of all, it was a day without a single carb craving.

The Diet

Chapter 83

After dinner she went upstairs holding the alarm clock. She felt full, satisfied and most surprising of all, energized.

The old sluggish feeling that she carried around with her day after day had been replaced with electric energy. She felt vital, too excited to sleep.

Her closet door was ajar, and Cate opened it wide and looked at all her clothes. There they hung from her smallest size sixes all the way to the oversized X's.

Uneasy neighbors, they were all mixed together, small next to big, skinny shoved up against voluminous, best-loved outfits jostling for space with functional body coverings. It seemed to Cate that they reproached her.

"I've given my kitchen a makeover," she thought. "It's time for my closet to get a makeover, too."

She stepped inside the space and began to pull hangers off rods, sweep sweaters and tops from their shelves onto the floor and tip boxes and bins out onto her bed.

So many clothes. So many memories.

The Diet

There was the pencil-thin skirt she was wearing the morning she did her pregnancy test; the first maternity top she bought, black with satin bows at the cuffs; a pair of jeans splattered with nursery paint; and the big tee shirts she had lived in for months.

"Time to be ruthless," she decided, following the two-year rule, separating out clothes she hadn't worn in more than two years to give to charity.

"Now," she said, looking at the piles of clothes at her feet, "how am I going to organize all this stuff?"

Then it came to her. She would organize her closet by size goals.

Cate made signs just like the stores had and hung them at the front of each size.

There was a sign for size six, one for size eight, one for size ten, another for size twelve, size fourteen, size sixteen, and then a big one for everything above that.

On each sign Cate wrote a date by which she would be wearing the next size, from the biggest to the smallest. Cate knew that she would wear each of those sizes again, until finally she would reach her size six and stay there.

When she was finished, it was deep in the night. Cate's bedroom glowed gently with the cool light of the moon and the soft light of her bedside lamp.

"What a difference a day can make," she mused. "Last night I was full of despair and ready to eat myself to death, and today I'm on my way to making my dreams come true."

The Diet

Cate flopped down on her bed and set her alarm. In her diet diary she wrote, "Dear D. D., I'm going to make it."

Then she closed her eyes, and lulled by the ticking of the clock, slept.

The Diet

Chapter 84

The shrill ringing of the alarm woke Cate up.

It was her first morning weigh-in.

A minute later, stripped to her skin, Cate stepped on the scale. It registered one hundred eighty-one-and-a-half pounds.

She stepped off and stepped on again. There was no mistake. She had lost five-and-a half pounds!

The Diet

Chapter 85

The days and the weeks flew by.

Every morning Cate's scale delighted her. The fat pounds she had accumulated dropped away, along with the fat inches.

At first she had worried that the first five-and-a-half pounds she had lost were water. After all, after a day or two, she had lost that much and even more on other diets. Then, on all those other diets, the same thing happened. The pounds became stubborn and refused to move. Worse, new fat pounds appeared. Disappointment and frustration and despair returned, too.

But not this time.

This time the pounds and inches left every day and every morning her scale marked their departure. They didn't come back. There was no disappointment. No despair. No frustration.

She lost as much in a week as she had previously taken a whole month to lose.

And the fat she lost stayed lost.

The Diet

Chapter 86

Her days were filled with fabulous food. She scoured all her old cookbooks, journals and note cards for recipes she could fit or adapt into her new A.M/P.M. food clock.

She shopped, cooked, baked, stirred and best of all sampled dozens of dishes. With every new dish, with every new menu, with every meal, Cate felt her body growing leaner, stronger, healthier and more vital.

And still the pounds melted away.

Now there was a rhythm to her days and her nights. Her body responded to this ancient rhythm and kept time with the gentle ebb and flow of sunrise and moonrise.

She was lulled by the gentle ticking of the clock. Each second measured her restored body, mind and spirit.

Day-by-day, meal-by-meal, Cate ate her way into a new body and a new life.

The Diet

Chapter 87

Every morning began with an adventure in fruit.

After her first sunrise orange she experimented with different types of oranges, from the thick-skinned navel variety, to the lighter-skinned Valencia, to the deep red of the blood orange.

When she got bored with oranges, she switched to tangerines and mandarins.

She tasted the wonderful essence of temples, a cross between the sweetness of an orange and the tang of a tangerine.

Sometimes she ate them sectioned and arranged on her best plates. Or she scooped them out, and filled the hollow skins with the chopped orange meat.

She cut them in half, sprinkled them with ground cloves and slid them under the grill for a hot and spicy morning treat she called Baked Orange Angels because they were so heavenly.

For a change, she baked apples and filled them with plump raisins and currants.

The Diet

She rediscovered pears and found to her delight they had the most cal-free carbs of almost any fruit.

She bought every variety; from the familiar Bartletts to the small Seckels, to golden Comices touched with rose, to the pale green Anjous and the deep earthy Boscs.

Some mornings she hollowed out her pear and stuffed it with a mixture of raisins and walnuts and added a sprinkle of lemon juice and a dash of artificial sweetener. She placed the stuffed pear in a small baking dish, with about an inch of water in the bottom, and baked it in the oven at 350°F for thirty minutes.

Then she showered and got ready for the day. When she was done, she broiled the pear for a minute or two, poured herself her first cup of fragrant coffee and took the first bite of her delicious baked pear.

Or she would toss together chunks of crisp apple, soft pear, juicy orange and a few colorful berries for a signature fruit salad that was endless in its variety and never failed to satisfy her craving for sweetness.

Sometimes she shaped a large Romaine lettuce leaf into a breakfast fruit cone and filled it with fresh berries, chunks of pineapple, mango or papaya.

She experimented. She ate. She lost. Pound after pound melted away.

Every pound and every recipe was faithfully recorded in her diet diary.

Chapter 88

Fast, simple and satisfying, breakfast became one of her favorite meals.

Gone were the mornings when she started her day with black coffee and ended up starving for carbs by ten o'clock. Now her mornings were a culinary adventure that took just minutes to make and enjoy.

She had come far from those first trial oatmeal cookies. Now she whipped up thick squares of breakfast brownies or a bread pudding using pieces of raisin bread soaked in milk, eggs, cinnamon and vanilla that was as rich as dessert.

She made waffles, pancakes and French toast and topped them with creamy sauces made with yogurt and fruit or spices.

She bought different types of cereals—bran flakes, wheat squares, corn nuggets—and mixed them up for her own special blend.

When she was feeling particularly ambitious, she baked breads and cut slices for her breakfast, enjoying them with her homemade strawberry, plum or bitter marmalade preserves.

As she learned how to shop for the cal-free carb she became even more selective.

As she shopped and learned, she kept losing.

Every purchase was recorded in her diet diary.

Chapter 89

Every morning, between breakfast and lunch, she filled up on more cal-free carbs.

Sometimes she would munch on dates, or chewy figs or even dried slices of apple or plums.

If she was feeling particularly festive she would make a morning parfait, filling a tall glass with combinations of her favorite fruit and topping it off with a big scoop of whipped topping and curls of dark chocolate.

All morning long, as Cate cooked and experimented with new recipes, she felt full and satisfied and content.

She knew that she had turned off the fat- making demons in her own body and was replacing them with energy-producing life.

The Diet

Chapter 90

Her lunches ran the entire culinary gamut from simple to exotic.

Some days she feasted on a chilled salad of baby shrimp and snow peas that were simmered in seasoned broth and garnished with the slightly bitter leaves of fresh celery.

On other days, she might broil a giant mushroom cup stuffed with a mixture of canned salmon and paper-thin green onions and seasoned with freshly ground pepper.

A favorite lunch was a combination of thinly sliced lean breast of duck, watercress and endive chopped fine, and crunchy chunks of water chestnut, all tossed with a special dressing of mayonnaise, yogurt, a little rice vinegar and, for an unusual touch, a teaspoon of raspberry jelly.

Cate turned the traditional breakfast of eggs and bacon into a wonderful lunch and added a pinch of curry or a teaspoon of chopped parsley to her scrambled eggs for a taste lift.

The Diet

She tossed together Caesar salads and topped them with marinated grilled chicken breast, shaved into slivers, and seasoned with freshly ground Parmesan cheese.

She made up her own version of the classics. Her chef's salad was heaped with strips of baby Swiss and English Cheddar cheeses alternating with thin slices of smoked ham and turkey breast and garnished with crumbled hot crisp bacon.

She always had a lunch soup simmering at the back of her stove. It could be a broth into which she swirled an egg until it thickened and floated to the top, where she sprinkled it with slivers of sharp green onion.

Or it could be a hearty French onion soup made with chicken broth and three kinds of onions and finished with melted Gruyere.

She experimented with thick soups heavy with chunks of beef or lamb or veal and shredded vegetables.

She ate and enjoyed and recorded every meal and every recipe in her diet diary.

Chapter 91

After lunch, she turned her attention to her afternoon snack.

Now her imagination and creative cooking skills had full rein.

She assembled her favorite cheeses and enjoyed chunks garnished with pickled onions or marinated mushrooms or crudités.

She even made her own cheese. Lining a large sieve with a coffee filter and pouring plain, nonfat yogurt into it, she set the whole thing into a large bowl so that the sieve didn't touch the bottom. She slipped the bowl into the fridge overnight, and the next day drained off the yogurt liquid that had collected in the bowl and turned out the thick yogurt cheese. Then she sprinkled it with salt and pepper and enjoyed scoops with her favorite raw vegetables.

She blended together cottage cheese with chives or olives for a savory filling for chunks of crunchy celery.

Or she added sweeteners and spices, like her favorite cinnamon, and turned the cheese mixture into ramekins for a snack as rich as a pudding.

The Diet

Chapter 92

She splurged at dinner.

One night it was a ragout, a savory one-skillet dish of veal, onions, tomatoes, peppers and pungent basil leaves.

She made a light-as-air broccoli and cheese soufflé with coriander and nutmeg that took only ten minutes to whip up and tasted as good as any served in fine restaurants.

She made Thai pork with honey and peanut butter and enjoyed the thick sweet taste of honey, the sharp tang of spices and the satisfying crunch of peanuts.

She grilled pork chops, serving them with tomato halves that she brushed with olive oil and sprinkled with Parmesan cheese, and slipped under the broiler for a minute or two.

Cate broiled steaks and sausages. She roasted turkey and duck.

She ate chicken every imaginable way, but her favorite was a classic roast chicken, with either an onion

The Diet

studded with two or three cloves or a quartered lemon inserted into the cavity

Cate didn't neglect fish. She created dish after dish that highlighted the fat-burning powers of the sea.

She folded slices of white fish, topped with fresh vegetables and drizzled with broth, into sheets of aluminum foil and baked them in the oven.

She baked assorted fillets of fish in a sauce whipped up from a little cream of asparagus or celery soup, a dash of skim milk, a little salt and pepper and a few teaspoons of shredded prosciutto or smoked ham. This was baked in a 350°F oven for just ten minutes for a hot, rich supper dish.

She made Sole Florentine, setting the cooked fish on a bed of spinach or Sole Almandine, sprinkling slivers of almonds over the fish.

With every dinner she prepared for herself, Cate became an exciting and inventive cook all over again.

The Diet

Chapter 93

The first week Cate cooked and ate and her scale rewarded her by recording a total of nine-and-a-half pounds of fat gone. She went down a full size.

By Halloween, Cate had eaten away sixteen pounds and was wearing clothes two sizes smaller.

She rewarded herself by scooping out a big orange and cutting a funny face in the skin for a miniature jack o'lantern. The rest of the orange she turned into something special. She processed the flesh until it was almost liquefied, mixed it with flour, baking powder, a little milk, eggs and sweetener and baked it into a hot breakfast bread.

Every day her energy and optimism increased.

"Surely Charles will respond this time," she hoped as she sent letter after letter. But they were met with silence.

Nonetheless, Cate kept going. She had a diet that was working for her, and she had a goal. She wouldn't stop now.

The Diet

As her weight decreased and her energy increased, she began to exercise. She started walking and then added muscle-strengthening and toning exercises from tapes she borrowed from the library.

The scale and the mirror rewarded her and revealed the real Cate emerging from her prison of fat.

By Thanksgiving Cate had lost another eighteen pounds and had become her own miracle.

To celebrate her progress and to give thanks she made a small traditional turkey, stuffing it with lemon, parsley, rosemary, onions, celery and a little salt and pepper. She rubbed its skin with olive oil and dusted it with a little paprika. While it roasted, she sipped a tomato cocktail sharpened with fresh horseradish and a dash of Worcestershire sauce.

For her afternoon snack, she placed curls of smoked salmon on thin slices of English cucumber spread with a little cream cheese.

She had lost almost thirty-five pounds in a little less than two months.

But still Charles was silent.

Cate spent Christmas quietly, never deviating from her diet or losing hope.

On the morning of New Year's Day, she weighed herself and found to her delight that she was just fourteen pounds short of her goal of one hundred and fifteen pounds. Cate had lost forty percent of her total body weight.

Just a few more pounds and she would intensify her efforts to reach out to Charles.

But as it turned out, Charles reached out to her.

Chapter 94

The first week of January Cate received two letters.

The first, from her lawyer, informed her that Charles had been offered a position out west and he was now pressing for a resolution to their situation.

The second letter arrived by messenger from Charles. Hoping for a reconciliation to mark the new year, he invited Cate to visit him the following weekend, which was in four days time.

Cate sent up a prayer of thanks. Her prayers had been answered. She won. She would get her husband back. She would get her daughter back. The bad times were finally over. Everything was going to be fine.

She was wrong.

The Diet

Chapter 95

"Not now, please," she begged the stubborn scale, "not now."

But there was no denying it. The scale didn't lie. For the first time in three months the pointer didn't move down.

Cate hadn't lost a single ounce, and she was still fourteen pounds from her goal.

"It's probably hormones," she reassured herself over her Rise & Shine broiled peach.

"It could be my period," she decided over her pineapple and pumpkin breakfast muffin.

By her morning snack, a pinwheel cookie stuffed with chopped raisins, figs and dates, she had decided to increase her exercise and set off for a longer, faster morning walk.

"Maybe it's stress," Cate reasoned over her chilled glazed salmon salad with a dilled mayonnaise dressing.

Then she took her second brisk walk of the day.

The Diet

Over her afternoon snack of mixed nuts and her dinner, a Mexican turkey casserole simmered in a rich tomato broth, embellished with sesame seeds, pine nuts, almond slivers, garlic, cloves and coriander and finished with grated unsweetened chocolate, Cate clung to the stress theory as the reason for the stuck scale.

"I've lost almost a pound a day. It's only natural that my body needs to slow down and adjust," she rationalized.

But all the reasons sounded hollow and desperate.

Cate fell into a troubled sleep, her dreams disturbed by visions of spinning scales and fat bodies without faces.

The Diet

Chapter 96

Through a thick fog of sleep she heard a loud bell ringing over and over again. Disoriented by dreams and darkness, she reached over, thinking it was the alarm clock. Then she realized it was the phone.

"Hello," she said, her voice raspy. She cleared her throat, pulled herself up to a sitting position, and tried again, "Hello."

"Hello, Cate, this is Charles."

Her heart started hammering. Could something have gone wrong? Was it the baby? She managed to keep her voice steady. "Is anything wrong, Charles?"

"No, I'm just calling to ask what time you think you'll get here Saturday. I'm leaving now for a few days for a job, and I won't be back until noon that day."

"I thought I'd try to get there by mid-afternoon, say around three o'clock?"

"Fine."

Cate drew in her breath to speak, but the phone was dead in her hand. Charles had hung up.

Cate tried not to read anything negative into his tone but some small part of her couldn't help wondering whether he was always so cold and punishing. She couldn't remember. Everything seemed tangled and twisted together with her fat.

Well, she was fat no longer and that thought cheered her as she got out of bed and onto the scale.

She couldn't believe it. She had gained back three of the lost pounds.

The diet was reversing itself. Cate's fat was coming back.

Chapter 97

Was it possible that the diet she had worked so hard to develop was going to be like all the others? Was it just a cruel and temporary glimpse into a slender, healthy future? Was she going to be imprisoned behind bars of fat once more?

Cate tried not to despair. She needed all her joy for this first meeting with Charles. She had to be happy, bright, and slender to get him back, and with him their child. She had to prove to her husband that she would be a wonderful mother and wife and that together they would be the perfect family.

She moved the scale to another part of the bathroom floor and tried again. Nothing. The new pounds were still there.

But for a brief moment, the fear melted away as she regarded herself critically in the full-length mirror. The scale might have disappointed her, but the mirror didn't.

She saw that she had almost achieved her goal. All that was left of the fat and swollen Cate of last year was a

The Diet

little thickness at the waist and a slight heaviness around the upper thighs.

Then her fears returned.

Instead of looking forward to those last few fat pounds and inches melting away, instead of looking forward to slipping comfortably back into the size six she had been most of her life, she was terrified. She was afraid that she would start to gain and gain and grow right back into her size twelves, then fourteens, then sixteens, eighteens and finally back into those plus sizes.

She began to sense that the body she had won back was betraying her. She could almost feel her fat cells beginning to swell once again.

"Don't be ridiculous," she chided herself. "There's probably some very simple explanation."

But she had no idea what it might be.

The Diet

Chapter 98

There they were.

Charles stood on the porch holding their baby. Cate could see Mrs. Bea's face outlined behind a twitching curtain.

She shut off the engine and stepped out onto the dry grass warmed by the sun of a mild winter day. It was warm enough not to wear a coat. Cate's sweater and tapered pants set off her newly slender figure.

She saw the guarded mask Charles wore over his features melt away, and he began to walk toward her. As he approached, he held the baby out to her. And Cate stepped into his smile.

Then she was in his arms, smelling his familiar scent, made even more comforting seasoned as it was with the faint fragrance of baby powder.

In that single moment it was as though everything that had happened since that disastrous dinner was a bad dream, a nightmare which had finally, blessedly come to an end. The demons were gone and Cate stood once again in a warm shining circle of love.

The Diet

"Cate, Cate," he murmured, "you're back. You're back. My slender, beautiful Cate is back."

She felt the rough wool of his sweater against one cheek and the soft downy feel of her baby's head against the other. It all felt so right, the three of them together, a family at last.

Cate silently repeated the pledge she had made to herself. "God, please restore my family to me, and I'll dedicate myself to Charles and our baby and never, never get wrapped up in my own selfish needs again."

Suddenly she felt Charles stiffen and pull away.

"What's that?" he demanded, looking through the open window of the car.

Cate followed his eyes to the front seat.

"Oh, that's my afternoon snack. I can't wait to tell you about the wonderful diet I created. I just eat and eat all day and the pounds and inches melt off, and Charles, I never felt better. Here, try some of these crab cakes."

She reached through the open car window, lifted out the container and held it out to him.

"You mean to tell me that you got thin eating?" he asked, his voice tight.

"Yes, that's what I want to tell you. It's a fantastic idea that really, really, works, and I think...."she got no further.

"You know what I think? I think you are just a food junkie. I don't know what you've been doing to yourself, but you didn't eat yourself into this body. And what's more, if you're on an eating binge again we're

The Diet

through. It's just a short trip from plastic bags stashed in the car to the fat cow you were. I'm not going to have my daughter exposed to that. I'm not going to risk having her turn into a food addict like you."

Cate stood frozen to the spot. She couldn't move. All she could do was watch as Charles turned abruptly away and strode back into the house, with her baby.

The Diet

Chapter 99

Cate sat in the car looking at the door closed to her once more. Behind that door was everything she loved, everything she wanted.

The unfairness of it all overwhelmed her. Why was she being punished this way? What had she done to deserve this? Why was she being shut out? Why was everything in her life failing her?

She longed for the love she once thought she had from Charles. She ached for her baby. She yearned for the life she imagined for so long.

But she could only satisfy the longing for food.

Reaching into the container, she began to eat.

Chapter 100

It was hours before she got home.

She was drained and exhausted. She had tried so hard, and she had lost. Charles, egged on by Mrs. Bea, would fight her for the baby and he would win.

In her despair she believed he was right. She had always obsessed about food and was still obsessing. She built her entire life around *The Cookery* and food and now food had betrayed her, not once but twice.

Her diet stopped working, and in four days she had gained back almost seven pounds.

Empty and filled with longings that couldn't be satisfied, she pulled into a small diner on a back-country road. She needed comfort. She needed food. She needed carbs.

"Sorry, the kitchen's closed," replied the solitary waitress wearing nurses' shoes, thick elastic stockings and a crooked name tag that identified her as Jewel. "Jimmy, that's our short order cook, went home sick an hour ago," she sniffed. "Kids," she added, clearly disapproving of

The Diet

anyone under the age of sixty-five who couldn't finish a twelve-hour shift.

Cate dragged herself to a plastic booth in the corner. She was the only customer.

"Say, are you all right?" asked Jewel, pouring her coffee and looking anxiously at Cate's pale face and trembling hands.

Cate nodded without looking up and raised the heavy ceramic mug to her lips with both hands.

"I could make you some eggs," the waitress offered.

She took Cate's silence for assent and came out five minutes later with a plate heaped with scrambled eggs and thick greasy slices of bacon.

"No bread left," she shrugged. "We had a bus load of antique shoppers through here early this morning and they cleaned us out."

Cate picked up her fork and lifted load after load of eggs and bacon to her mouth. She ate without tasting.

"I knew all you needed was a little food," said Jewel as Cate paid her bill. "A skinny little thing like you needs to eat more."

For the next five miles Cate laughed hysterically at the irony and the pain in those words. Then she wept.

Chapter 101

It was over.

She had lost the battle for her family, and now she was losing the battle for her own body.

How deluded had she been all those weeks, thinking that she had some magic solution, when all the experts tried and failed to find a perfect diet?

She opened the door to her house, walked straight down the hall and into the kitchen and opened the fridge.

She was bathed in light once again. She wasn't alone, not when food could keep her company.

Why should she bother any more? She had lost everything that mattered to her. She was a failure.

Cate was sick of trying, tired of the roller coaster ride from fat to thin, from hope to despair.

Nothing had changed for her since that night Josh dumped the pizza and files and check into her arms. That money was gone.

Glancing down at her flat stomach, Cate knew she was going to lose her body again. She also knew that she couldn't stand it a second time.

The Diet

She thought of calling for her old friend pizza, but it was almost midnight and the place was closed. Everything was closed.

The only comfort left was in her fridge.

So Cate looked at the two plates she had prepared, one for her and one for Charles. What a stupid fantasy that had been, Charles coming back here.

Together, they would watch the baby sleeping in the middle of the big bed and then slip down to the kitchen to enjoy a late supper of slices of grilled steak marinated in lime juice Over dinner they would make plans for their future.

Well, that fantasy would remain a dream. There was no beautiful baby sleeping in the middle of her bed. There was no kind, attentive husband sharing dinner and dreams with her.

She took out the dinner she had prepared for them both and ate the whole thing herself.

Tomorrow she would go shopping for ice cream and cookies and candy. Why not?

Upstairs, the closet door stood open, revealing the size sixes, her final goal. She slammed it shut and threw herself sobbing on the bed, stuffed to bursting with food.

The Diet

Chapter 102

The next morning, Cate opened her eyes to a dark and gloomy day and the infernal ringing of the alarm clock.

Cate had lived her life to the sound of that clock for months and up until yesterday every ring meant that she was getting one meal closer to her baby and her husband.

She picked up the clock, walked it into the bathroom, and tossed it into the trash.

Then, from force of habit she stepped on the scale. "Just once more," she thought, "and then I'm going to throw the scale into the trash right on top of the clock."

She glanced down. It wasn't possible. She had lost seven-and-a-half pounds overnight!

She stripped off the clothes and jewelry she had fallen asleep in and gingerly stepped back up. It was true. She had lost all the pounds she had regained over the past few days since her weight-loss got stuck, and an extra half-pound, besides.

Chapter 103

"How is it possible? What did I do differently? What did I eat yesterday that I didn't eat before? What triggered the pounds to come off? What got me unstuck?" she asked herself.

She ran down to get her diet diary and flipped back to the pages for the day before.

The first entry was a cold baked apple, sliced and topped with a spoonful of lemon yogurt.

For breakfast, she had had a muffin torte, a thick chewy bran muffin sliced into six thin layers, each layer spread with alternating plum, apricot and strawberry preserves and then reassembled.

Her morning snack was a treat. She indulged herself with a sundae, a big scoop of no-sugar vanilla ice cream. She made a hot strawberry topping and garnished her sundae with chocolate sprinkles.

Lunch was a creamy omelet seasoned with salt and freshly ground pepper and swirled with a little chopped parsley and finely diced smoked ham. Folded, topped with grated Cheddar, it was slipped under the broiler until the cheese bubbled. She had cut up some tomato wedges, drizzled them lightly with a little extra virgin olive oil, and tucked a fresh basil leaf on either side of the dish.

She turned to the page for her afternoon snack. It was blank, as was the page for her dinner.

Cate tried to reconstruct exactly what she had eaten and when after her last entry.

She remembered the disaster of the afternoon snack—the crab cakes—but she couldn't remember eating them. She hugged her robe tightly around her and went out to the car. The container on the front seat was empty. She must have eaten the whole thing.

She wrote the snack down in her diet diary.

Then she remembered her double dinner, the scrambled eggs and bacon and the two portions of sliced steak. She added them to her diary, too.

"So what was different?" she asked herself. "What had unstuck the scale? What had emptied my body of fat while I slept?"

Staring at the diary pages, she saw the answer, the final piece to her perfect diet.

The Diet

Chapter 104

It was so simple, so common sense, she wondered why she hadn't thought of it before.

Her whole diet had been based on synchronizing her meals to the constant rhythms of time, but there was one major element of time she had completely ignored.

She had been faithfully eating meals high in cal-free carbs in all the A.M. hours of the day. The result? She had successfully shut off her body's fat-making switch.

She had been faithfully eating meals high in fat-burning protein in the P.M. hours. The result? She had successfully raised her resting metabolic rate to burn off her old stored fat.

She went back to her diary. This time, instead of looking at *what* she had eaten, she looked at *when* she had eaten.

The Diet

Chapter 105

The key was in what she had eaten the night before and when she had eaten it.

While she had been eating cal-free carbs in all the A.M. hours of the day, she hadn't eaten fat-burning protein in all the P.M. hours of the day.

It made perfect sense.

For months and months, she had eaten her dinner, her last meal of her diet day, around seven o'clock in the evening.

The next meal, her Rise & Shine, was twelve hours later. Then she would shower and get dressed and have breakfast at about eight.

That meant that there was just one hour between her first morning meal and her second. Sometimes breakfast would be a little delayed, but usually there was no more than an hour or an hour-and-a-half between her first two meals.

Then she would have her morning snack sometime between ten and eleven o'clock.

The Diet

Again, the time between breakfast and her next meal was usually no more than three hours.

Depending on her schedule, her lunch would be anywhere between noon and one or one-thirty in the afternoon.

The time between her morning snack and her lunch was never more than two hours or so.

Her afternoon snack was enjoyed between three and four, depending on her schedule, her mood and her hunger.

There was only three hours between lunch and her afternoon snack, and some days even less than that.

She ate dinner around seven o'clock, three or four hours after her snack.

Then she ate nothing for twelve hours.

Was it possible that her body, believing that dinner was her last meal for twelve hours, was shutting down over night, refusing to burn fat, and what was worse, starting to store it again?

The Diet

Chapter 106

She had believed that she was safe from new fat being formed while she slept, but she wasn't. When she had a lot of fat to lose, the momentum of losing had kept the pounds dropping off. As she got closer to her goal, the momentum slowed, until finally it stopped. Without the extra metabolic boost, it had begun to reverse itself, and the lost pounds started coming back.

There was something else.

Why did she believe that she shouldn't eat anything after dinner? Didn't her body keep burning fat for those few after-dinner hours until she went to bed?

What did she think happened to her metabolism, to her fat-fighting powers while she slept?

Did they sleep, too?

She kept breathing all night long. Her heart kept pumping through the night. Why should she neglect to keep her body working to fight fat overnight?

Last night she ate the sliced steak close to midnight. By eating another meal before bed, she shortened the time between meals. There was no time for

The Diet

her body to go into starvation mode and start making new fat.

Like so many others, she believed that breakfast was the most important meal of the day. It wasn't.

Her most important meal of the day was a bedtime snack to keep her fat-fighting cells going all night long. She could wake up leaner than when she went to bed.

It had already happened.

She would add a bedtime snack to her diet. She wouldn't get fat again. Her diet wouldn't be just half of a twenty-four hour day—it would be the whole day and the whole night.

There was hope. She wasn't going to give up.

Food was not the destroyer. Ignorance was. Fear was. Despair was.

She would never again be ignorant of how her body worked, of how it turned food into fat and fat back into energy.

She would never be afraid of food again.

Food had been her life once and it would be again.

The Diet

Chapter 107

A few days later Cate was back to her best weight of one hundred and fifteen pounds.

In those few days, she had added an after-dinner snack to her diet.

There were golden eggs stuffed with creamy, whipped cottage cheese, dotted with chives, or seasoned with flecks of paprika.

She made a hot soothing gratin cooked in a small ramekin, bubbling with eggs, tender spinach, thick cream and melted Swiss cheese. This she placed on a lap tray decorated with a bud vase and a single rose, and ate in bed.

Sometimes she rolled thin slices of ham and turkey and chicken breast around logs of thick yellow cheese and garnished her bedtime deli platter with seasoned nuts.

But her favorites were the desserts she created with sweetened and flavored cheeses.

There was an amaretto cheesecake and one dotted with pecans. There was a rich dessert of creamy cheese piled into parfait glasses or crystal dessert dishes. She even made cheese cookies to take to bed and enjoy with hot chocolate.

Every evening her body glowed with vitality.

Every morning her scale rewarded her.

She had done it.

She had found a way to eat and lose with all the food she loved.

And she learned that the food she ate hadn't changed. She herself had changed.

Chapter 108

It was time for Cate to write again. She sat down at her kitchen table with her diet diary and a small laptop.

Cate was going to write for herself and for her baby. The two of them, her and Charlie, would be the family she would fight for.

Her weapons would be food and words.

Going back to her beginnings, she would become a writer of food once again. Josh needed a new food writer. He was going to get one.

And so she began.

She wrote how food had turned on her and betrayed her.

She told the story of her mother who lost her life to her carb addiction and junk food and the tragedy of her sister who died taking chemical shortcuts to weight loss.

She wrote about losing *The Cookery* and the babies she gave birth to, one dead and the other snatched from her.

The Diet

She didn't leave out the pain she felt when she finally realized she had lost her husband and all her hopes for having a family with him.

She wrote about losing her book contract and her career.

She recounted that terrible night when she sat at her kitchen table, almost two hundred pounds of her, waiting for her carbs to arrive, determined to eat herself to death as fast as possible.

She wrote about opening the door and seeing Josh and how ashamed she felt.

She confessed to dropping the armful of folders and pizza and eating the slices right off the kitchen floor.

Then she wrote about reading that one headline in an obscure study that talked about cal-free carbs.

She conveyed the excitement of that night, all the work she did, the research, the adventure of developing an idea.

She wrote about praying for a sign and how the little card with the picture of the multitude feasting on the loaves and fishes fell out of her mother's cookbook.

She shared her belief that cal-free carbs and protein were the two halves of a perfect diet and how her alarm clock regulated her meals through the hours of the day—A.M. for cal-free carbs and P.M. for proteins.

Then she told about her frustration when she got stuck and how eating not one but two dinners guided her to the idea of a bedtime snack.

The Diet

She felt stronger and more powerful with every word, especially when she described how health returned to her body and to her spirit.

She wrote about how it felt to get control over her body and how it felt to get her life back.

Finally, she wrote down the diet.

When she was finished, she shoved the printed pages into an envelope, put on her coat and drove to Josh's office at the *Record*.

Chapter 109

"Cate, this is really great stuff," Josh exclaimed as he turned page after page.

"I can't believe how amazing it is that you put all this together and that it works so well. Obviously, it does. You look terrific."

Cate soaked up his praise and his admiration like a thirsty sponge. It had been a long time since she felt like she accomplished something worthwhile. It had certainly been a long time since any man had looked at her the way Josh was looking at her now.

"Can you give me more of this? More recipes? More menus? More research on this incredible cal-free carb?"

"Sure. Yes. Of course. When do you need it?" Cate asked.

"Are you kidding? Yesterday would be good," Josh said, in the manner of all newspapers editors everywhere.

Then he put down the pages and reached across the desk and folded her two hands into his. His skin felt warm and dry, and a pleasant shiver ran through her at his touch. "Welcome back, Cate. You were missed."

Cate turned her head so he wouldn't see the tears of gratitude for the first kind words she had heard in months.

She left Josh busily editing her copy.

Filled with faith in herself, she drove home through the early evening twilight, certain in the knowledge that she would get back her daughter.

For the first time in a very long time, Cate felt peace.

Chapter 110

Cate heard the pounding on her front door, alternating with sharp bursts of the doorbell. Confused and still groggy with sleep, her first thought was the baby and without even taking the time to throw on her robe, she flew down the stairs, burst through the front door and tumbled right into Josh's arms.

"Cate, take look at this." He shoved a copy of the *New York Morning Sun* at her.

"Josh, what am I looking at? What is it?" she asked.

"This." He turned back the front page and there she was, a full-page picture of Cate next to her story.

"That's not all," Josh went on. "I've had calls from all three morning shows, two network news shows and four talk shows. They all want you. I've fielded interview requests from reporters from just about every major paper and even a couple from Japan and one from London."

She wasn't taking it in. It was overwhelming.

"But Josh, how—I don't understand," Cate said, shivering in her thin nightgown.

The Diet

"Here, let's get you inside," said Josh, wrapping her in his jacket.

"Make us some coffee and I'll tell you the story of a woman who turned to her soul to save her body. It's your story, Cate. It's all you. I just added a couple of file photos to what you wrote and sent it out over the wires."

Chapter 111

Standing in the chilly morning, wrapped in Josh's jacket, Cate saw happiness and pride in his eyes, and something else. She saw love.

Cate wasn't cold any more.

She tossed the newspaper high into the air so that the sheets flew and tumbled in the morning breeze and reached out and took his hand.

"How about one of my special Rise & Shine recipes, something I could whip up just for us," she said with a mischievous lilt in her voice.

Smiling, she led him through the door.

The Diet

The Diet

Part Three

The Diet

The Diet

Chapter 112

It was October once again. The leaves had crisped to the warm golden bronze of freshly-baked cookies.

"You look and smell delicious," Josh said, lifting a damp curl off Cate's neck and replacing it with a kiss. "You taste good, too."

Cate's shivered with delight.

"I want seconds," and he grabbed Cate's waist and brushed her warm skin again with his lips.

"Josh," Cate laughed putting down the long-handled slotted spoon she had been using to carefully skim the foam from the simmering consommé, "that tickles."

But instead of moving away, she leaned back against him, filled with contentment, as he wrapped his arms around her.

She felt his warmth against her back. She felt blessed. Her life had been restored to her.

"It's almost the end of another year," said Josh.

"Yes, October is supposed to be a month where everything comes to an end," Cate replied, looking out through the large kitchen window at the garden and the golden trees beyond. "But for me October is more than a month of endings. It's also a month of new beginnings."

Josh rested his chin on her dark curly hair.

She and Josh were married and living in a house they restored deep in the country.

They stood together at the gallery-sized window in the huge kitchen. Warm and beautiful, the kitchen was the beating heart of their home and their family, because, at long last, Cate had her family.

Charles, with a new job on the other side of the country, had abandoned their child as easily as he had once abandoned Cate.

Cate's daughter came home to them. She and Josh christened her Anne Samantha after Cate's mother and her sister. Charlie, the name she had been given in the hospital, was forgotten.

Cate and Josh stood quietly together, feeling the beating of each other's hearts and listening to the ticking of the battered old alarm clock that stood on their kitchen counter.

"Josh, everyone's going to be here soon," Cate reminded him as she squirmed out of his grasp. "It's four o'clock and I've still got the whole dinner to finish, and you," she said turning to give him a kiss on the cheek and raising her hand to touch his face, "you've got to get the table and chairs organized outside."

"Okay," he agreed, and walked over to Annie. He picked her up from her little play enclosure, swung her over his shoulders and carried her across the back lawn where they would have their last dinner of the year under the stars.

"I wonder what this October will bring?" she mused. "Will it be an ending or a beginning or both?"

Chapter 113

The kitchen was warmed and misted with puffs of scented steam escaping from under the lids of bubbling pots.

Tonight, Cate and Josh were giving a dinner, a celebration feast. The occasion was the announcement of Cate's first book and the naming of the successful company that would win the right to publish it.

Cate had become a star.

She had her own cooking show, a monthly feature in a national magazine, and, of course, the weekly columns in the *Record,* which found their way into over three hundred newspapers around the country.

But what she didn't have was a book, not after what had happened the last time. Not after *Middleton & March* and of course, Gena.

But publishers and literary agents had been quick to recognize her commercial value as a new celebrity, and not a week went by when she wasn't flooded with book offers.

The Diet

Middleton & March was the first. They thanked her for the repayment of the previous advance and began to court her again. They sent a young, sleek acquisitions editor who shrugged when Cate asked him what had happened to Gena. He hinted that should Cate decide to pick their bid, the previous six-figure contract could now go as high as seven figures.

Others followed.

It was Josh who had come up with the idea.

"Let's have a kind of silent auction," he suggested after fielding yet another call from an eager publisher. "I'll let everyone know that if they want to publish your first book, they have to send in a sealed bid. We'll have a big dinner in the garden, open the bids, and pick the winner."

Tonight was the night.

Cate had come full circle.

On her kitchen desk was a very neat stack of sealed envelopes, each containing an offer. The top one, which had arrived by special messenger that morning, was from *Middleton & March*.

The Diet

Chapter 114

She was happy. She was cooking.

Cate turned down the gas under the big soup pot of consommé, stirring it lightly to blend the rich veal stock and dark cloves that gave it its steaming fragrance.

Next, she turned to the sink, sending a shower of cold water over the tubs of glistening fish, butterfly shrimp and rough-shelled clams, washing them free of sand and small scales.

At the last minute, she would toss the fish and shellfish into a tomato, onion and garlic broth seasoned with a drizzle of olive oil, bay leaves, thyme and an exuberant dash of cayenne pepper. She would serve this adaptation of savory Cioppino, the legendary San Francisco fish stew, in a big tureen.

She had already seasoned the chili con carne with coriander and cumin, and had thrown in her secret ingredient—a few sticks of cinnamon—and set it to slowly simmer on a back burner.

An old sideboard, stripped down to its pale pine base, held the desserts.

The Diet

A dozen raspberry cheesecake parfaits in slender glasses stood on a large silver tray. Sparkling with pink and gold, the bright layers of raspberry purée, crushed almond biscuits and a creamy blend of ricotta and cottage cheeses were finished with a scattering of raspberries and a cap of whipped cream.

Beside them she had set a platter of fat strawberries dipped into darkest chocolate.

There was a big glass bowl filled with colorful melon balls waiting to be spooned into wide-mouthed glasses and topped with Champagne or ginger ale and garnished with pungent sprigs of fresh mint.

In the freezer, a pan of pomegranate crystals froze into an unusual autumn sherbet.

Cate stood at the oversized chopping block, stripping all but the very tops from a huge bunch of fresh rosemary. Making her own version of Shashlik, a Russian dish, she would thread cubes of pink lamb that had been sitting in a bath of honey and lemon zest onto each rosemary spear and grill them.

Hands fragrant with herbs, Cate had just started on the lamb when the doorbell rang.

The doorbell rang again.

Josh, deep in the garden, was too far away to hear it, so with a quick glance at her pots to make sure they wouldn't boil over, she grabbed a dish towel and ran to open the door.

"Hi Cate. Remember me?"

It was Gena

Chapter 115

Cate remembered.

She relived the first rush of pleasure when Gena told her she was an executive editor at *Middleton & March* and offered her a book contract and the terrible day when that contract was cancelled.

And Cate remembered the sheen of tears in Gena's eyes when she told Cate about her own lost career.

"I remember, Gena," replied Cate, opening the door wider. "Come in."

But Gena made no move to enter.

"Cate, I just wanted to come by to say how very sorry I am about everything that happened. I wouldn't have wanted to hurt you for the world."

Cate looked at her more closely and saw a very different woman standing in front of her. The old, brash Gena with all the hard edges was gone. A softer, more tentative Gena stood outside her door.

"It was a long time ago," said Cate and then stepped forward and hugged her old *Cookery* class student.

The Diet

"Oh, Cate," said Gena, her voice tight with tears as she gave Cate a hug in return.

"My pots! I've got to turn them down," laughed Cate. "Come on into the kitchen." She led the way with Gena following.

"How have you been? Where have you been? What have you been doing? You just dropped out of sight," said Cate, tossing a pinch of oregano into the chili and giving it a quick stir.

She turned to Gena.

"You know, there's something different about you. Something quieter. I remember you always carried that huge tote and that enormous briefcase and that phone of yours—it never stopped ringing. Where is all that stuff?"

Gena carried only a small clutch in her hand and a single manila envelope tucked under her arm.

"Don't mind me," Cate continued, turning back to the stove lifting lids and stirring pots.

"We've got a kind of celebration planned for tonight and I'm just putting the finishing touches on dinner. You are most welcome to stay."

"I know about the dinner. That's why I've come."

Something in Gena's tone made Cate turn around and look hard at her.

"I've changed, Cate. I did a lot of thinking after they made me cancel your contract and ask for your advance back and then fired me. I hated myself that day and I hated *Middleton & March*."

"So what are you doing now?" asked Cate.

"I've started my own publishing company."

"That's wonderful."

"I thought it would be. I imagined that all I had to do was empty my bank account and pour my life savings into a fancy office at an impressive address. After all, I was one of the top editors in New York. I was really good at spotting winners. I made millions of dollars for *Middleton & March*. I thought I could do the same for myself. I could be my own boss, make my own rules.

"I was wrong. *Middleton & March* were furious, and they have a very long reach. No one would talk to me, much less sign with me." Gena's voice broke. "I'm out of money. I'm scared all the time. And I've never felt so alone in my whole life."

Cate took a step toward her, but Gena backed away.

"Look, I really shouldn't be here. Not after what happened. I was crazy to come. Desperate actually. I just wanted to give you this."

Gena handed Cate the manila envelope she had been holding tight against her body.

Cate took it, raising her eyes in a question.

"It's my bid. I heard about your auction. I would like to publish your book. I know that a dozen publishers have approached you, including *Middleton & March*. I can't offer you anything like they can," said Gena quickly.

"In fact, I can't offer you anything at all. I don't have any money for an advance. But I can promise you that you can write whatever book you chose. Write it

The Diet

exactly the way you want, with no interference at all. I can promise you that."

Stunned, Cate needed time to think.

"Are you still interested in old Americana cookbooks?" she asked gently. "I found two wonderful examples at a flea market. They've got some great early American recipes in them. Go on, they're on the coffee table in the living room. Why don't you pour yourself a glass of wine and check them out?" she motioned to the tray and glasses standing ready on the counter. "It's almost time for dinner and of course you'll stay."

"Thank you Cate," Gena said, pouring herself a glass of wine and following Cate's direction to the living room

Alone again, Cate placed Gena's envelope on the desk on top of the one from *Middleton & March*.

The Diet

Chapter 116

Everything was ready. Cate just needed a few fresh vegetables, and she liked to leave those to the very end, gathering them minutes before serving. She picked up a large flat basket and went out to harvest the last of her kitchen garden.

It was tucked into a sheltered elbow under the tall windows of her kitchen.

There were rows of carrots, beets, potatoes, and onions. Thick vines of cucumbers, squash, melons, peas and beans curled along the ground and twisted around the wooden stakes and frames that supported their weight.

Bushes of blackberries as well as raspberries, now stripped of fruit, grew against an old fence and jockeyed for space with towering sunflowers.

Borders bloomed with fall flowers: yarrow, dahlias, zinnias and asters.

Huge terra cotta pots brimmed with tomatoes and all her favorite fresh herbs, from chives to tarragon.

The garden had been Cate's own special project. Refusing any help, she had planted it herself. She toiled

The Diet

over it, breaking up the heavy clumps of earth, smoothing and shaping the rows that would hold her seeds. She fed it, watered it, cared for it.

As Cate pulled up the last of the round, firm onions, as she played hide-and-seek with a stray cucumber and a handful of autumn beans, as she filled her basket with sun-warmed tomatoes and freshly-clipped herbs, she thought about her garden.

Its bounty had blessed her and her family all summer long.

She crushed a mint leaf in the palm of her hand and breathed in its clean sharp fragrance.

Cate knew about herself and food. She trusted herself.

She would never again be afraid of food.

She would never again be controlled by food.

She would never again deny herself food.

Instead she would rejoice in it.

Once, food may have been the cause of her near destruction. But now, as she breathed the deep, earthy smell of the fresh vegetables in her basket, she knew that food had brought her to a new life. Food had become her redemption.

The Diet

Chapter 117

Cate brought her basket inside. Smiling, she looked around her kitchen and at the food she had prepared.

Once again she owed her life to food, but this time to a diet she had created.

She thought about all the food diets her mother had been on and all the chemical diets her sister was a secret slave to. She remembered all the diets she had chained herself to. Every diet had failed them.

Diets had meant such disappointment, despair and ultimately death for those she had loved.

Diet. How that word had terrorized her. But a true diet, a real diet, wasn't denial or suffering or failure or death.

Diet was linked to food and food was linked to life and life was love. That was the real food chain.

Chapter 118

It was almost time.

Cate sat down at her kitchen desk for a few minutes and looked at all the framed pictures arranged on its surface.

As she looked at each one she thought again about beginnings and endings, about coming to terms and about finding peace and love.

Cate looked first at the picture of her mother and remembered not the mother who lay dead on that stained kitchen floor, but a younger, happier mother standing at a stove, stirring and tasting and laughing with Cate's father. She remembered the glow of the kitchen and the tinkle of the lids as they danced on the pots. She also remembered a funeral. Her father disappeared. Her mother's smile faded away, and the kitchen never glowed again.

Cate now understood that her mother had turned to food in her loneliness. Food had comforted her, and then wouldn't let her go. Cate understood because she had done the same thing. She was linked to her mother

The Diet

through their common search, diet after diet, hoping against hope to find the one that would release them.

Cate remembered the night her mother's hand had touched hers and guided her. Unable to save her own life, her mother had saved Cate's.

Cate reached across time to her mother and loved her again.

She looked at the picture of her sister Sam, the long wind-blown blonde hair, the eyes crinkled up against the sun, the tiny slender body.

Cate had been so angry with Sam for dying and leaving her alone. But it was Sam who had been really alone.

Sam had been a diet victim, too. Terrified of food and controlled by that terror, Sam had sought her own perfect diet in secret. She thought she found it in dangerous shortcuts. But she didn't. She lost her life instead.

"Oh, Sam," Cate thought, stroking the frame that held the image of her sister, "I'm sorry I was so angry with you for so long. I'm not angry any more. I miss you. I love you."

Cate opened the desk drawer and took out the picture of Charles she had placed there face down.

Thinking about him, she understood that he was weak and frightened.

She had blamed him for their failure.

But when their marriage experienced its first sharp test, both of them had pulled away from each other. The

The Diet

bond of loss that first bound them to one another proved too weak to hold them together.

It was time to bring them together again.

She set his picture among the others. He was Annie's father. He had been her husband. He had been part of her life. She had loved him. He belonged there among the gallery of faces on her desk.

She lightly touched the framed card of the loaves and fishes that now sat in the center of the desk, in the place of honor.

Cate thought about the Bible story that showed her the first link between food and love. She thought about the higher power that gave her a body to feed, a mind to exercise and a soul to nourish. Cate recognized what extraordinary gifts those were and that she must care for them as they cared for her.

Finally, she looked at the waxed rosewood frame that held her favorite picture of Josh and Annie. He was sprawled in a wide Adirondack chair under a willow, his face partly shaded by an old straw hat. Annie, holding a bunch of crushed and bent wildflowers, stood on his lap.

It was from him she first learned what love really was. He loved her for herself, not for what she looked like or how much she weighed or what size she wore.

Josh would love her for a lifetime, and she would match his love with her own. But she would do more. She would keep herself healthy, slender and strong to make sure the lifetime they shared could last.

Opening a small box that had been sitting on the corner of the desk, she took out a small white porcelain frame. It was empty, but in a few months it would hold the picture of her new baby. She set the frame on the desk with all the others.

The Diet

Chapter 119

The garden burst into a thousand stars that seemed to dance up every tree and bush. Josh had turned on the fairy lights and transformed their garden into a magic place.

Josh saw her in the window and waved. He was holding Annie in his arms and moved her little hand in a wave, too.

"Can I help with anything?" asked Gena, coming into the room.

"Not yet, thanks. Give me a couple of minutes. I'll call you. Go on outside and enjoy yourself."

Cate watched as Gena walked outside and stopped to talk to Josh. She saw Annie run up and tuck her hand into Gena's.

They looked right together. Annie and Gena. Baby and book, forever linked.

And then Cate knew what she had to do.

The Diet

Chapter 120

Cate picked up the envelope Gena had brought her. She broke the seal and slid out the single page, read it and smiled.

"Write anything you like," Gena had said.

Cate picked up a pen and a sheet of paper and wrote:

To my mother
To my sister
To my daughter
To my unborn child
I dedicate my first book
I call it The Diet.

Then she reached into her apron pocket and took out a small picture. It was a recent photograph that Josh had taken of her. Smiling, she placed the photo on top of the page she had just written.

With that gesture, Cate began to love herself.

The Diet

Author's Note

The Diet Cate developed for herself, while fictional, has some basis in research. Much has been written about the weight-loss effect of protein. The zero-calorie carb, cal-free carb and non-stick carb are all names for dietary fiber. Research shows that dietary fiber is indeed a carb with virtually no calories of its own and passes through the digestive system unabsorbed. There are also indications that dietary fiber may play a role in obesity. Keen-eyed shoppers will notice that many food labels have added dietary fiber to their lists and subtracted the fiber carbs from total carbs.

For more information on these and other nutritional, exercise and health topics please visit the following sites:

National Institutes of Health
National Academies of Science
American College of Preventive Medicine
Food & Drug Administration
American Heart Association
American Cancer Association
American Dietetic Association
To name only a few...

Information & Ordering

Mail
Send check or money order for $24.95 U.S. funds only. U.S. orders please add $8.95 for shipping and processing. Non-U.S. orders please add $15.95 for shipping and processing.

The Diet
830-13 A1A North
Ponte Vedra Beach, FL 32082

Retail
The Diet is available wherever books are sold.

Online
Please visit our website at www.dietnovel.com.

Bookstores
Please order through Ingram or Baker & Taylor.

Bulk Sales for Organizations
Please contact the publisher directly via our website at www.dietnovel.com.

Coming Soon
Please visit our website www.dietnovel.com to see what's coming up next and to reserve your copy of upcoming books.

The Diet